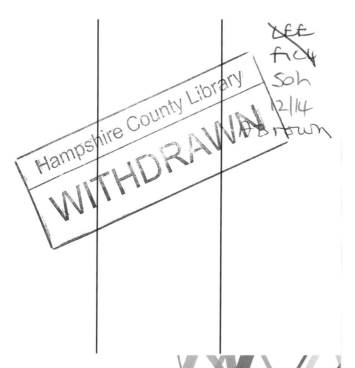
Get **more** out of libraries

Please return or renew this item by the last date shown.
You can renew online at www.hants.gov.uk/library
Or by phoning 0845 603 5631

Hampshire
County Council

"Wyatt, what is it?"

The next she knew he was against her, his mouth burning hot and rough against hers. Not the way she'd imagined their first kiss. Caught so off-guard she could do little more than react, she let her arms come up under his as he steered her backward to the wall and ground her into it, kissing her with the length of his big body.

She'd always liked kissing—good, wholesome fun kissing. This was nothing like the playful, gentle kisses she'd found on the lips of any other men. It overwhelmed her, burning away every other thought, claiming every part of her—it was a flow of something hot and molten that dragged her down, burning her lips, singeing her tongue, searing her from the inside out with his breath she breathed.

When he lifted his head she could only stare at him, light-headed and shaking, her arms still locked around his shoulders, broad, warm, and steady...and she couldn't think of anything but kissing him again.

Imogen tried to get control of her breathing, but held fast lest he get any ideas about letting go before she got her balance. *Say something. Quick!*

"I like the way you talk" was what came out, followed by a bubble of semi-nervous giggles.

Smooth.

His gaze fell heavy on hers. Dark. Troubled. Though the giggles ceased, words still failed to materialize—and she was usually so good at talking.

Dear Reader

Growing up, I shared a dream typical of kids growing up in the country: I wanted nothing but to see the world. I didn't expect the way that travel would affect the way I see the place when I come home again, letting me really appreciate the lush beauty of the Appalachian region and the rich local culture of the kind, generous, and colourful people who live here.

I'm so happy my debut novel allows me to introduce this place to those who will never walk these wooded hills, explore what home really means, and tip my hat to the notion of finding love in the most unexpected places.

I hope you enjoy reading Wyatt and Imogen's story as much as I enjoyed writing it.

I'm thrilled to hear from readers. You can find me online: amalieberlin.blogspot.com, www.facebook.com/amalie.berlin, or by e-mail—amalieberlin@gmail.com

Cheers!

Amalie

CRAVING HER ROUGH DIAMOND DOC

BY
AMALIE BERLIN

First published in Great Britain 2013
by Mills & Boon, an imprint of Harlequin (UK) Limited,
Large Print edition 2014
Eton House, 18-24 Paradise Road,
Richmond, Surrey, TW9 1SR

© 2013 Darcy Gafeira

ISBN: 978 0 263 23871 6

Printed and bound in Great Britain
by CPI Antony Rowe, Chippenham, Wiltshire

There's never been a day when there haven't been stories in **Amalie Berlin**'s head. When she was a child they were called daydreams, and she was supposed to stop having them and pay attention. Now when someone interrupts her daydreams to ask, 'What are you doing?' she delights in answering: 'I'm working!'

Amalie lives in Southern Ohio with her family and a passel of critters. When *not* working, she reads, watches movies, geeks out over documentaries, and randomly decides to learn antiquated skills. In case of zombie apocalypse she'll still have bread, lacy underthings, granulated sugar, and always something new to read.

I dedicate this book to my mom.

For enduring months of tears and tantrums
while teaching this dyslexic girl to read.
And for tricking me into reading of my
own free will (at 11) with an old 1960s
Harlequin® Romance™ and the warning that I
was only allowed to read this *grown-up book*
if I took the responsibility seriously…

CHAPTER ONE

THE PROSPECT OF six months in rural Appalachia pinched like a noose around Imogen Donally's neck. Three months—four, tops—was how long she liked to stay anywhere. Six months may as well be six years.

Amanda was the only person she'd even consider such a request from, and then only because she hadn't seen her in a couple of years and Amanda's need was great. Her pregnancy had started smoothly, but a week ago there had been an incident and now Imogen's best friend—her only long-standing friend—was on bed rest for her entire third trimester. Single motherhood was hard enough without those kinds of complications. She needed help. In that perspective, six months wasn't so long, right? Less time than gestation...

She took a deep breath and engaged all-terrain on her four-wheel drive, eyeing the deeply trenched gravel drive supposedly leading to the forested mountain home of Dr. Wyatt Beechum, Amanda's cousin and boss—owner of a modern medical oddity: his family practice was housed on a bus.

This looked like the right place. Unless the hand-painted numbers nailed to a tree meant something other than the street address. Amanda's directions were written in her usual wandering fashion: mentioning every landmark along the way. Mile markers on the road. The number of bridges she'd cross. And Imogen's personal favorite—indications of where things used to be. As if Imogen had any clue where things used to be around there. She wasn't even sure she could find things where they were currently located.

And yet, when asked for the insights into Wyatt that Imogen needed to plan her approach with him, the usually talkative Amanda had been tight-lipped. Recently returned home for his father's funeral after years and years away. Lost his mother and brother when he was young. The traveling clinic was in danger of losing funding. Sad stuff, but not very telling. None of it especially helpful. So it came down to charm and playing it by ear. Her plan was simple: find the doctor; charm the doctor; and get him to let her cover Amanda's maternity leave.

He needed a nurse to help keep his two-person

traveling practice going, so he should be happy to agree. Easy-peasy. Just as soon as she drove up this creepy, dirty, graveled incline into a dense forest.

She reached for her phone. No signal. No double-checking the location with Amanda.

This dark forest drive was probably quite normal for the area. Every new place required a certain amount of adjustment. She just needed to acclimatize. Nothing scary waited at the other end. No crazy hillbillies with too much moonshine and chainsaws awaited her. Just a man. A normal man. A doctor, she hoped. She could handle one measly doctor. No problem.

She got a run at the incline. Better she stalk him here than at work. The car bounced up the path, now and then hitting potholes large enough to jar the fragile glass mementos packed in the back. Not hard enough to break them. They were okay. Not that any sane person should be so attached to cheap trinkets.

Six months from now, she'd get back on the road and life would return to normal. Any time she stopped moving too long, someone expected her to stay forever. Imogen couldn't do forever. Besides, that wasn't going to happen this time. She and Amanda had lived together all through college, and they had both survived parting. If only the world had more Amandas.

Dr. Earp, as she'd come to think of him, should be glad she was willing to head down to Banjoland to help out. Excellent nurses available on twelve hours' notice were hard to come by.

A shiny black pickup sat in front of an old blue school bus with curtained windows. Someone lived here, or was here at least. Beyond it, she could see the beginning stages of a cabin. It was only a few logs high, but connected to a beautiful riverstone chimney.

Praying the rise in elevation had given her a signal, she reached for her cellphone again. She'd even take one stupid bar. Was it too much to ask for enough connection to send a text? Apparently.

She killed the engine, checked her hair to make sure she looked fairly presentable, and climbed out. Behind the cabin, lying parallel to one another up the slope, were several long straight trees. As she rounded the bus, a man came into view, looking all sorts of rugged and manly. Black hair, disheveled and longer than the white-collar type she had been expecting. Worn blue jeans. Work boots. White T-shirt. Handsome. And tall. Very tall. With safety goggles.

Which was when she noticed the chainsaw.

The man jerked the cord to send the blade whirling and angled it into one of the logs. Wood chips flew everywhere as he made a series of shallow cuts, and Imogen went unnoticed. Must be the safety goggles obstructing his vision.

Not emotionally ready to approach a big mountain man with a chainsaw, Imogen occupied herself by checking her presentability again in the dusty bus windows—which seemed more important now that she'd seen this broad-shouldered man with a chainsaw. Streaks of pink in her pale blonde hair stood out like beacons. Out of place. Oh, well, maybe it'd make her exotic. And after the hot contractor told her where she could find Wyatt, he could take her out for drinks and help her pass the next six months.

And maybe he could also explain to her why she could see a bed and old console television between the gaps in the bus curtains.

The outrageously loud buzzing quit, drawing Imogen's attention back to the rugged outdoorsman. "Hello?"

No answer. Instead, he took his shirt off, balled it up and used the wad of material to brush from his corded bronze arms the tree shrapnel he'd created with the chainsaw.

Probably not Wyatt. That tall, broad-shouldered man with the back of a chiseled god could not be him. The only doctors she'd seen with their shirts off had been pasty and usually somewhat pigeon-chested. The profession didn't naturally lend itself to buffness. Probably why she always ended up with the rough-and-tumble lot. They looked good, and were rarely given to the deep, soul-baring conversations you started building forever on. Imogen knew that road. Dead end. Full of potholes. Kind of like the road on which she'd just driven up the mountain.

She started up the incline, which got his attention. Their eyes met through the scratched plastic protecting his eyes. That probably should've made the experience less exhilarating, but Imogen found herself smiling like an idiot and resisting the urge to toss her hair and add extra wiggle to her walk. "I'm looking for Dr. Wyatt…something. You're not Wyatt, are you?"

He extracted earplugs and stuffed them into his back pocket. "What do you want?"

Well, that was a crappy greeting. But that's okay. With those shoulders, Tall, Dark and Cranky could work for her. "I'm looking for Wyatt Beechum... B. E. E. C. H.... Actually, I don't know how it's spelled."

He dropped the now still chainsaw to his side, letting it dangle as he impatiently spelled *"Beauchamp"* for her then repeated, "What do you want?" Hot contractor had bad people skills.

And might not be the contractor.

"I don't think that's right. That's all...French and whatever. This is like the tree, maybe? Beechum."

"That's how it's said around here," Likely Wyatt muttered. "Guess no one saw fit to modify the spelling."

"Oh. Well, I'm Imogen, a friend of Amanda's." She stuck out one hand and approached, ready to shake and be friendly.

"I know. My cousin is a picture hoarder. Has you in several on her walls." He looked at her hand, but didn't shake it. Which was better than being chainsawed at least—which might be the only way she'd feel less welcome. She could only pray his bedside manner was better.

"I'm going to assume you're Wyatt and not another cousin lurking about." On the plus side, working with him would give her plenty of time to convince him to show her the sights. And anything else he wanted. He was taciturn enough that he didn't seem inclined to long talks about his hopes, dreams, and future two point five children. She could just pretend he was mute as long as his shirt was off.

"I told her this morning you should've called before wasting the gas."

"Okay." Her nose wrinkled and she paused, needing a mental kick to get her back on the reason for her visit. "You filled the position already?"

"No, but you can't help me."

"I'm a good nurse." She started with business, seeking common ground.

"Amanda said as much. But you can't be her replacement."

"Her temporary replacement." Imogen corrected that first, still smiling, though now with effort. "If you know I'm a good nurse, and your usual nurse recommended me, why do you say I can't help you?"

He pulled off the goggles and laid them on the log he'd just notched. "No offense, but Amanda has the respect of the people we care for, and no matter how good you are at your job they won't trust you and won't be as open as we need them to be to get the best care."

"Seems a little last century to me. You're afraid I can't take care of people because they speak with a different accent than I do?" She smiled, trying to cajole him. "I can do the accent if that's seriously your hang-up."

"Don't try to do the accent." He leveled a stern look at her, as if he could stare the words into her with those dark eyes. "You're an outsider. You'll never be someone they'll identify with. I can't use you."

To buy time to think, Imogen walked the short distance to inspect the cabin walls. "You're local. Can't they just talk to you as a trustworthy insider, and I'll follow your lead?"

"I've been gone a while. They're not sure what to think of me yet."

She tried a different tactic. "That's not the bus, is it?" That ancient wreck wouldn't inspire anyone to come and get healthy in it.

He didn't say anything, just gave her another wilting look, then went about maneuvering the first log of the line.

"Good." This really wasn't working out the way she'd pictured, and she dearly wished he'd put his shirt back on. She never had trouble making friends. Everyone had some kind of common ground, the trouble was finding it. "Do you need help with that?"

"No." He grunted the word more than spoke it, but, then, he was obviously exerting himself, wrestling a log to the cabin walls. The muscles across his shoulders and down his back bunched, momentarily wiping her mind of anything clever to say. "I don't need anyone's help with the cabin." He didn't stop working to talk, though he may have been slowed down by it.

"Go visit Amanda, your trip doesn't need to be wasted."

"Later." She walked up the embankment as he continued with his logs. Once she stopped the lusty staring, some cognitive function returned. "Do you think you could put your shirt back on? Wouldn't want you to lose a nipple in a tragic log-rolling accident." She failed to suppress her natural cheekiness. Impulse control: sometimes she had it, sometimes she didn't.

He smiled up at her—his first smile since she'd arrived—and immediately lost his balance, nearly falling. It took skill to regain his footing and keep the log from getting away from him.

Okay, she was cute. He didn't want to like this pink-haired woman. Couldn't afford to like her.

Liking her would make him more likely to grant her request, and he needed to make all practice-based decisions with a clear head. He'd had his fill of do-gooder city doctors as a kid when Josh had been sick, and he'd sooner close the practice than have it turn into a professional pit stop for conde-scending outsiders. No matter how cute.

"I've been doing fine without the running com-mentary so far." He'd also been doing fine without shapely tanned legs drawing his eye away from his work. Doing better, really. He changed posi-tion so she stood between him and the old blue bus. He never liked looking that direction, and the change made it easier to pay attention to what he was doing rather than to her legs.

"Okay." Up until now, she'd been mostly good-humored about his refusal, but her continued pres-ence said she wasn't the type to go down without a fight. Strange that she and Amanda were such good friends—they couldn't have been more dif-ferent.

"I can see you want to get back to work," Imo-gen said to his back, "so I feel obligated to point out that you can get rid of me very simply. Say you'll let me work the next few months, and I'll leave you to play with your big-boy building logs in whatever state of dress you like."

She didn't talk like a nurse. They were usually a little more cautious and obliging than this one. She really didn't like being told no. That was tough. "Find a job in Piketon if you're sticking around." He got the log close to the cabin then used rope to muscle it into position.

"They don't need me in Piketon. Like it or not, you do." She moved into his line of sight again and propped her hands on her hips, looking more confident and at home on his mountain than she had any right to. "You can't run your practice by yourself, and Amanda's made it clear how uncertain its future is. Funding in jeopardy and all that business. She wants her job back when she's able, and that means there needs to be a job for her to go back to."

The cuteness was starting to wear off.

Wyatt dropped the rope and looked at her, keeping the bus at his back. Winter would be here before he knew it, and the cabin needed to be roofed before then or he might be staying in the blasted bus. That couldn't happen, and wouldn't if she'd go away. "Kicking up a fuss won't win me over.

Glad you came to help Amanda out, but you aren't working for me."

He briefly considered paying her to leave, anything to make her stop looking at the bus. Damn, that thing needed to be gone.

The fingers on her hips dug in and she looked from his chest to his neck, to his eyes, then off to the side. She was tall. Tall enough that even with his height and the additional elevation where he stood, she still came up to his chin. Must scrape six foot, this one. For some reason it pleased him to find her struggling with where to look at him.

"You're not even going to give me a chance?" Her body language screamed discomfort, but she wasn't backing down. Something else he didn't want to like about her.

Maybe if she stuck around, in a couple weeks—after he hired someone—he'd visit and make amends. No matter how bad a fit, anyone who'd drop everything to run to the side of a friend in need deserved respect at least. "There's no chance of this working."

"You don't know that."

"I do, actually. I've seen this scenario play out many times when out-of-town medical professionals with good intentions come to help the back-

woods mountain folk. I know you mean well..."
Even when they'd spoken jargon they'd mistakenly assumed a child wouldn't understand, he'd known they'd meant well. And he'd known how sick his brother had been. Good intentions never saved anyone.

"I do mean well." She pushed her hands into her hair, dragging it back from her face as she finally looked back to his eyes. "Give me a chance. If I fail, fire me spectacularly and smooth over any feathers I inadvertently ruffle. I can give you references. I have more accreditations than you'd believe. I've worked in all kinds of different places. I can adapt."

He shook his head once more and his answer finally took. With much muttering to herself, she stomped off down the hill. There wasn't much he could make out, but the word *"ass"* came through loud and clear.

Probably fair. He heard the car door slam and the engine roar to life, and glimpsed her purple car before losing it in a cloud of dust that told him she was tearing down his mountain faster than was safe.

Purple four-by-four. Pink hair. She should work in some upscale cosmetic surgery center, not in a mobile clinic traveling through the neediest, most remote communities in the Appalachians. Sure, she might spend a couple weeks there doing charity work, especially if there was a mine explosion or some natural disaster, but she'd always go home before long.

Imogen definitely wouldn't fit in, and she couldn't even if she tried.

It was too bad. She looked fun to play with. At least, when she stopped talking.

Finding a place to turn around took forever. It was a good half hour before Imogen made it back up the fool's mountain. She shouldn't have let him run her off. Failure was not an option.

She marched straight for Wyatt and the look he gave her was a mixture of irritation and surprise. But his shirt was back on, thank God. It helped her keep the steam she'd built up in her aborted departure.

He opened his mouth to say something. She shushed him preemptively. "You just listen. I'm going to help you today. The only way you're getting me off this mountain is by calling the cops. I'll wear you down. I'm like…" She blanked, blinked, and hurried past it. "Something that wears people down." Analogy failure wouldn't stop her either. Imogen waved her gloves at him.

"Got my tire-changing gloves. Put on my boots." She turned her foot out to show him those too. "If at the end of the day you can still say I'll be no help, I'll leave you alone." And just as she got to the end of her tirade the analogy crystallized and she blurted out, "Water! I'm water. I'm *so* water, and I can move mountains if I keep at it. And you're just like a mountain. All tall…and unmoving."

"Okay, Water. It's a nice offer, but—"

"But I can't help you. You said that already," Imogen cut in, trying to keep the shoulder-tensing frustration out of her voice. "Do you always make snap judgments about people?"

"I listen to my instincts."

"And your instinct says?" She gestured impatiently for him to spit it out.

"Friendly. Cute. Unreliable. Insubstantial."

Maybe she gestured too impatiently.

"Insubstantial? Good grief." She retrieved a hairband from her pocket with such a rough touch it snapped her knuckles, the sharp sting wrecking her impulse-control efforts. People usually kept their masks polite, but Wyatt came at it backwards. If his mask was this surly and unpleasant, did it hide something worse?

Focus. His opinion only mattered as far as it affected her ability to cover Amanda's leave. In six months she'd be gone and he wouldn't matter anymore.

"Okay, give me a chance to prove I'm substantial enough to get the job done and then—as much as I think it's ridiculous for a man to play with chainsaws all by himself in an area with no cellphone coverage—I'll leave you in peace at the site of your future, accidental amputation." Okay, so maybe she should've been trying harder to keep the frustration out of her words and been less worried about her tone.

"No." Wyatt stepped over the stumpy wall and made for the logs again. "And no standing within fifty feet of the cabin."

"You should wear gloves. Don't you know doctors are supposed to have soft hands?" She thrust her gloves at him, refusing to abide by his fifty-foot decree. "Want mine? They aren't seeing any use now."

"I'm fine."

With a grunt and a shake of her head Imogen dragged the gloves on and followed him. "I'll help you by dragging the logs to the cabin, and you won't have to wait so long to run your beloved chainsaw. Give me the rope."

"No."

Hadn't the man figured out yet that she wasn't going to leave until he said yes?

"It's hard work. You'll hurt yourself," Wyatt added.

"The last place I worked was at a pediatrics unit." She dropped her gloved hands to her hips, instantly aware of how stiff the gloves were. "Want to know what I learned there?"

"No."

"Too bad! I'm telling you anyway." *Ass.*

"You really don't like being told no, do you?"

Wyatt actually chuckled a little then, but it was the kind of mirthless, superior man noise she noticed happening at those times the little woman tried to do man's work—like learning to change spark plugs. Or move logs. Having drinks and passing the time with this man no longer sounded like much fun.

In fact, the urge to hurt him nearly overwhelmed her already limping impulse control. "I learned that if you want something and you're told no, you should do other stuff that they don't want you to do. Worse stuff. Until they reconsider your first, sensible request. Or you should just keep asking until they give up from exhaustion."

He tied the rope around the notched end of the log and straightened, giving her a weird, almost amused look. "How often that work for you?"

"I'd say about three out of four times. People don't like confrontation." She amended, "Most people."

"There's nothing you can do on the mountain that will bother me enough to change my mind." He looked at her a long moment then turned, pulling the rope over one shoulder to drag the former tree down to his cabin.

The man clearly had no idea how annoying she could be if she set her mind to it. She almost regretted him putting his shirt back on. Pine cones and prickly seedpods from the sycamores would be great for proving to him and his stupid amazing back how irritating she could be.

Imogen followed, barely resisting the urge to pelt him with prickly tree bits, her mind in a mad scramble for another way to handle him. Amanda didn't want someone getting comfy in her job while she was away, and Imogen was the pit bull she'd chosen to turn loose on the problem.

But maybe she'd set this up wrong from the start when she'd made it sound like a request. He was under the illusion she was the one who would eventually give up from exhaustion. Or maybe firm but sensible would work where bratty and frustrated had failed.

"Please?" Please should help, at least a little. "I'm invested in this working," She tried to keep her voice as level as possible—no easy task considering she was one of the people who generally avoided confrontation. Confrontation meant getting involved in subjects that caused big feelings and crossed lines she didn't like to cross. "Give me a chance to prove myself. Or say yes. I'll leave and see you tomorrow for work, Dr. Beechum."

"So…" Wyatt looked her fully in the eyes, somehow making her feel short for once. A little intimidated. That's the reason people liked to avoid confrontation. Uncomfortable. "Your offer to help move logs is to annoy me into saying yes to hiring you for the practice?"

"Um, no. Maybe that's how it looks, but offering to help was not to annoy you." Imogen rubbed her head with the still stiff rawhide glove. "That was a different plan to make you say yes. That plan involved showing you that I'm a quick learner."

She began ticking off fingers as she talked herself up, but the gloves were so stiff her ticking lost the pizzazz she'd hoped to muster. "I'm determined to make it work. I'll work very hard to make it come out well for everyone, including your patients, Amanda, and even you."

Wyatt looked at the gloves and back to Imogen's face. Nice face, even all pink and angry like that. Her help—anyone's help, really—was the last thing he wanted. If Josh had survived, they'd have been rebuilding together. As the last Beauchamp standing, the responsibility was his alone.

"You really are like erosion." Exceptional at wearing things down. Absolutely relentless. "If it will make you shut up, go ahead. You won't make it ten minutes, but move the logs if you're able." She wouldn't be any help. Letting her wear herself out on a log might just get her out of his hair.

He grabbed the chainsaw and safety gear. Before starting it, he watched how she did with her first log. Stubborn woman. No way in hell was she going to get that thing moving without hurting herself.

The rawhide gloves she'd been bandying about looked to have never seen use. Still stiff and not a mark on them. She flexed her fingers a couple times to get them bending then mimicked what she'd seen him do earlier: turn, rope over the shoulder, then lean forward to pull. A few aborted tries and she choked up on the rope, which lifted the end enough to actually get it moving. Stronger than she looked, and smart.

The shorts were impractical for that kind of labor, but it let him see her legs flex from her calves all the way up to a plump little rear. Hard to look away from. Since he'd come home, Wyatt had resisted all the local attempts to fix him up. But now, with Imogen's legs and rear distracting him... Swearing off dating since he'd come home might not have been the best decision.

Shake it off. Get back to work.

Imogen worked as long as she could. But even taking a break after every log, her whole body still hurt. Her shoulders screamed the loudest, like a foghorn warning her away from the dangers ahead. She had a new appreciation for packhorses and whatever farm animals had to do this in the olden days—before she'd been around to make stupid points about being a hard worker.

She flopped onto the ground where Wyatt

marked more logs to cut, sprawling gracelessly on her back. "Okay. I admit it, this was a dumb idea."

Wyatt chuckled, and it sounded like honest amusement this time. "They're heavier than you'd think."

"And I..." Her voice cracked. She swallowed and tried again. "Can't remember what I was going to say."

He pulled a watch from his pocket. "You've been at it a few hours. I need to make a call. Think you can make it to the ridge?"

"You want me to climb the mountain with you?" Oh, sure, now he wanted her to go somewhere with him. Now that she couldn't move.

"Yes."

For once he didn't say no. If he were a puppy, Imogen would give him a treat. More yeses was what she wanted to encourage in him. Plus, hard workers didn't lie down on the job, though they might ask for help to get up. She lifted one hand toward him. "If I fall, just cover me with leaves or something suitably survival-oriented."

His hand was large and warm, and were she not exhausted, Imogen would've sworn her skin buzzed where his touched it. Distracting, and prob-ably due to her poor, overworked hands having to grip that rope so hard for so long. Even if the universe was dead set on punishing her for her stubbornness, at least Wyatt seemed to have softened to her a little. Enough to be cordial, if nothing else.

Once she was upright, he released her hand, waited for her to get a drink, then started up the steep incline. A shorter stride and a slower pace said he was waiting for her to keep up, probably another nod to cordiality. The air no longer crackled with irritation, and Imogen wanted to keep it that way. She tried to move faster than she actually wanted to move: zero miles per hour.

When she resorted to using the trees to slingshot herself further up the incline, Wyatt backtracked and took her by the hand to haul her the rest of the way up the hillside. "Not in the mood to chase you down the hill when you start rolling, or to carry you to the hospital when you fall and crack your head open."

"So gallant," Imogen murmured, but she held fast to his hand—grateful not only for the assistance but for the distraction his touch provided. The sensation wasn't buzzing, though it had a kind of vibration to it. It was more like an energy she couldn't identify. Waves of tingly awareness raced up her arm and to distant, interesting parts of her body. Parts that now demanded more attention than her screaming muscles. If he could keep this Helpful Polite mask on, she might revisit that drink idea.

"Big step." Wyatt dragged her attention back to climbing then took both of her hands in his and hauled her the remaining few feet, past the tree line to the grassy ridge.

When she was steady, he released her, fished out his cellphone and strolled a short distance away, leaving her to take in the view.

Imogen folded back onto the ground, her eyes tracing the contours of the rolling green hills that spread out in front of her. "Okay, the view was worth the hike on screaming limbs."

"Thought it was a good reward."

He sounded distracted. She glanced his way and watched him scowl at the phone in his hand. "Trouble?"

"Need a new one…" He tapped the screen a few more times and shook his head.

"Want mine? It's the toughest of cellphones. Waterproof. Easy to use. When you can get a signal, that is."

"Why do you have a waterproof cell?"

"Sometimes I get caught in the rain with the top off my car."

He shook his head, but the small smile made it less judgmental. With her phone in his hand, he took a few steps away to make his call.

She should definitely take a picture when he got done. Also maybe take a picture of him and his whole chiseled-muscles thing. Hard. He was probably hard all over. If only he was less mentally hard. Short-sighted. Narrow-minded...

He was probably thinking the same thing about her. Which was fine. If it got her what she needed, he could think what he liked. She already had a friend, and one was plenty. The last thing she needed was to impress another member of Amanda's family and have them start comparing notes on her. Or conspiring to make her stay.

He kept his voice low, but she could hear the tension in it as he spoke.

"So you have to climb a mountain to use a cellphone around here. Sort of negates the convenience factor." Talking to herself, another sign she was tired, crazy, or that maybe it was time to give up. As she gazed over the scenic panorama, she caught a glimpse of something white in her peripheral vision. On a flat spot inside the trees down the ridge sat lots of big white blocks placed in a rectangle. She waited for him to hand back her phone and asked, "Did you start building up here first?"

"No…" He didn't need to look where she was pointing to know what had roused her curiosity: the barrier wall surrounding the old family grave-yard. She didn't need to go there. Best leave that undisturbed. She disturbed enough on the moun-tain without turning her loose on the dead too. "That's not a house foundation. You had enough of the view?"

"Picture, then I'm done."

Having confirmed the agency couldn't get a suit-able replacement by tomorrow, he'd best consider whether or not to brave the week alone or give her the shot at the job she repeatedly demanded.

Wyatt waited at the trees for her to get the photo and rejoin him. Her feet dragged—not nearly as much bounce in her step as when she'd haughtily stormed his mountain—but she didn't look so close to dropping as she had when he'd hauled her with him up the climb. "Need help?"

"No, I'm better." Betterish, maybe. She stuffed her phone into her pocket and took the kind of deep breath a person did when about to attempt something requiring concentration.

He helped her off the first ledge-like step anyway, then let go. A few steps down and he turned to look back at her, needing reassurance she wasn't going to fall after he'd worked her like a mule all afternoon. Her own fault, too stubborn to stop when it had got to be too much, but he'd feel bad if she got hurt because he'd let her exhaust herself. He'd never thought she'd actually pose a threat to his rule about the cabin or he'd just have put the earplugs back in. Why hadn't that occurred to him earlier?

Was this what it would be like to let her work for him? Someone he'd always needed to keep an eye on wouldn't be much help. As nurses were always in demand, it made them hard to get on short notice. Amanda's opinion of Imogen counted for something, but he had to wonder if part of her support was just friendship or knowing how fast Imogen would be available. But in his experience, annoying and stubborn were easier to suffer than superior and condescending. Having her work for him might even make him look good enough by comparison that he'd become the one the patients opened up to, rather than his nurse.

His shoulder cracked against a tree, forcing him to look where he was going again. "If you need help, say something."

"I will," she called, her voice labored and breathy.

No, she wouldn't. She'd set her mind on proving she could work herself half to death and suffer no ill-effects. Who could deny Wonder Woman a job?

Maybe he'd been a little premature on the insubstantial label. She was substantial enough to fight for what she wanted.

"I'm fine. It's a little easier going down. You just have to kind of control your fall by using the trees. They're like nature's speed bumps."

It was the nature's speed bumps bit that got him. He laughed out loud, surprising himself, and lost his footing. The second time one of her quips had cost him his balance. His legs shot out from under him, and he did precisely what he'd been worried she'd do.

He fell down the mountain.

CHAPTER TWO

IN THE SPACE of a few seconds Wyatt traveled several yards down the mountain and was caked from hip to heel with a layer of dirt. Some time during his impromptu trip the outside of his right forearm had caught against something. It hurt.

"Wyatt!" Imogen shouted his name twice before he sat up. "You're bleeding."

"It's okay. I'm okay." And just as soon as he finished a mental inventory of his parts and aches, he'd believe his own words.

She knelt and lifted his arm to look at the gash he knew was there.

"Wow, whatever got you must have been sharp. It opened the skin right down to the fascia. Muscle doesn't look cut. You don't have a scalpel in your pocket or something, do you? Open pocket knife? Broken glass?" She slid her fingers into his, keeping his arm up and stationary so she could get a better look at it. "It needs stitches."

"Hard to conduct myself when I'm watching

someone else," he muttered. Stupid. Of course he'd have to fall in front of her. And now that her fingers were linked with his, he realized how small they were, fine-boned and delicate. How in the world had she managed to move the logs at all? Her slender fingers didn't look strong enough to flex the stiff gloves, let alone haul timber. She may be tall, pushy and annoying, but her hands were soft. Feminine.

"Yep, you should've kept your eyes in front of you and let me fall if I was going to. I said I'd yell if I needed you." Imogen wiggled her fingers free and shifted her hands to the hem of his shirt, which she tugged. "Take off your shirt. Need pressure on that and I'm not taking off mine."

Another travesty.

"It's not covered in mud?" He looked at himself again, shrugged and raised his arms so she could lift the shirt. Her little hands shook—just the barest tremble—as she helped him out of his shirt.

"Do I make you nervous?"

"Oh, yeah. Earlier with the chainsaw and now I'm afraid that I might ogle you, and that's hardly professional." She smiled at him and teased, but he recognized a bedside manner when he saw it. Her voice had changed. Her whole demeanor had changed. The words may be teasing, but the tone was sweet. Much sweeter than she'd shown him so far. Distracting him from the pain and humiliation, and doing a damned fine job of it too.

"Not that it'd be my fault," Imogen added, helping him up. "I'm sure you spent years bench-pressing fallen trees just so you could make annoying women babble at you when you fall off mountains." She flipped the shirt inside out and gently wrapped his arm. "Pressure here. Try not to jostle that, there's grit and debris in the wound. You think a speck of dust in your eye hurts…bits of dirt and wood in an open wound would be torturous."

Half an hour later Wyatt sat in the passenger seat of her ridiculous purple vehicle, instructing her through town. His little town wasn't particularly secluded, not like the communities he drove the practice to, but it still took time to get there from the mountain. But it took no time to get through the tiny town to the large lot where his big shiny silver bus was parked.

A much better bus than Dad's. Getting that wreck off the mountain would give him the incentive to get the cabin built. It just meant going inside first to get stuff. Pictures. Mom's jewelry box. The family bible. Dad's crossbow. Important stuff. The only problem? Wyatt didn't want to go inside.

"This isn't the hospital," Imogen said, dragging his mind back.

"No. It's my practice." He popped the car door open and stepped out, closing the door again with his knee to keep the pressure on his wound. "Keys, right front pocket."

Imogen looked at the jeans pocket and then back up at his eyes. The fact that he was standing there, shirtless and bleeding, demanding she fish around in his pocket after he'd spent the day repeatedly refusing her requests registered. "It's locked." And his arm hurt, but he wasn't going to admit that. He added a word to avoid admissions. "Please."

She crammed her hand into his pocket and retrieved the keys. "Which key?"

He indicated and she let them inside.

"Why are we wasting time here?"

"We're here because it's close, it has all required medical supplies, and there's no waiting." He followed her, bumping the lights on with his good elbow. "First exam room, you'll find everything we need in the cabinets."

Imogen went ahead of him, doing as he'd bid, but obviously not happy about it. "This is silly. I'll clean it, dress it, then we'll go to the emergency room. You cannot suture the outside of the forearm on your dominant hand. And, yes, I noticed you're a righty."

Time for her to kick up another fuss. If she wanted the job, she'd prove it. "That's why you're going to do it."

"I've never sutured." She grabbed supplies and then headed to the sink to wash up. "And it's kind of illegal. I'm an RN, not a PA. Actually, it's illegal for you too."

"After you glove, wash my arm from the elbow down. Then irrigate with the saline and grab a mirror from the third drawer so I can see it."

"All that I can do. It's legal."

Her thoughts played across her face so clearly she might as well have said them. She thought he was testing her.

Of course he was testing her.

"I bought the supplies. This is my practice, and you don't work for me," Wyatt murmured as she set about cleaning his arm. "You're just a friend I'm trusting to help me out."

"You have funding. Didn't the funding buy these supplies?"

Smart. But also cautious and a little too reticent—traits that wouldn't serve her well around here.

"No. I haven't actually acquired funding yet." Another test. One that stopped her cold.

"Amanda said you were in danger of *losing* your funding." She lifted her gaze from the wound and stared at him with the biggest blue eyes he'd ever seen. Big blue eyes with a smudge of dirt under one. It was good his hands were occupied because he had a sudden urge to thumb the smudge away.

She had to stop staring at him like that. Made it hard to focus. She was probably experiencing the same thing. He was making the tests too hard.

"That's what I told her, and if you're her friend you won't tell her different." Her mouth had fallen open with surprise. Wyatt tilted his head to try and see what she was doing as it was the only way to keep from staring at her mouth. He coughed. "She wouldn't accept her full salary if she knew it came from me and not from a fund."

She started moving again. Despite her suspicions and the long day, her hands moved steadily and gently over the wound. "So, this is a regular practice? That stuff about getting the use up…"

"That's true. There is funding available if I can get the patient base big enough. Until then…" She should smell terrible. He knew he smelled awful after the long day, but she smelled good, and she'd worked herself hard—probably to the point of dehydration.

She dried his arm after flushing the wound and checking under magnifying glass for any debris. Whatever her thoughts about his revelation, she kept them to herself. "It looks clean to me, but I still wish you'd—"

"You want me to trust you. Show me I can." He reached out with his other hand, making contact with her forearm. Whatever strange chemistry rumbled between them, she felt it too. Her gaze fell to his hand, compelling him to take it away. "Today I saw a hard worker, someone who wants to help. Now show me someone who is willing to take the same chance on me that she's asking me to take." Wyatt smiled, trying to soften what amounted to a dare.

"That's not the only problem. You're trusting me to do this right without any practice. I've never so much as stitched up a turkey for Thanksgiving." Imogen held the mirror up so he could see the wound. Seeing it made it sting worse, but she was right—flayed to the fascia. Should be easy to stitch.

"If you can follow directions, you'll do fine. If you mess up, I'll go and get new sutures put in tomorrow. But if they're good, I'll give you two weeks to prove you can handle the position."

"I thought I'd already proved myself on your mountain." Imogen pointed an accusing gloved finger at him.

"I never said yes." Antagonizing her before making her stitch him up might not be the best idea he'd ever had, but he'd rather she snapped at him than a patient. "I just let you move the logs."

Her eyes called him an ass again, but to her credit she bit her tongue.

"You were being very annoying," Wyatt said, and when she scowled, he held up one hand, "But I can now see your bedside manner is different." When she still scowled, he corrected himself. "It's better. Good."

"A month. That's the bare minimum required for a fair trial," Imogen countered.

"Is it?" Wyatt couldn't help but grin at her. She was ballsy, and that was something people here would respond to—it was easy to respect bravery. "One month, unless you do something so terrible I can't keep our arrangement. Behave, and don't annoy my patients."

* * *

He was the cousin of her best friend, and they were close. Close-ish. Imogen wasn't entirely certain what that entailed, but it didn't matter. He might be kind of a jerk, but she had to believe he wouldn't do something to ruin her life. Oh, sure, he might not hire her because she allowed herself to be talked into doing something illegal, but the chances were slim that he intended to jeopardize her license.

Imogen wanted to say no, be as uncooperative as he'd been all day. She'd learned how to be stubborn the last time she'd held still for six months. But being flexible might actually get her what she wanted. Unless he tried to trick her again.

She considered his expression, saw nothing but sincerity there and sighed. Like she had a choice. She wasn't built to leave someone suffering if she could help them. Leaving him with an untreated injury just because he ticked her off… Couldn't do it. And she couldn't go halfway on her promise to Amanda—she made promises so infrequently already.

"I suppose we should numb it. Where's your pharmacy? And tell me what to give you." If the stitches were crooked, loose or too far apart, it was his own bossy fault.

He rattled off directions and sent her packing with his keys to a locked cabinet for drugs and a suture kit. Not even a flinch when she gave him the injection. He just started explaining how to work the needle and the kind of stitch he wanted.

Imogen drew a deep breath and picked up the instruments. She'd seen this done a million times. She'd removed stitches a million times too. No problem. It was just like repairing a hole in her favorite dress. If her favorite dress happened to be made out of human flesh. Ugh. Amanda had better have booze at her house left over from her non-pregnant days.

The first stitch seemed to take forever. Imogen realized she was wincing in tandem with Wyatt's frowns. She tried to relax her forehead, a tension headache brewing between her eyes. "Looks straight." A slight tug tested the give, and when it looked decent she allowed herself another deep breath, "One down. How many do I need to do?"

After looking at the cut again, he asked, "How many do you think?"

"Six? Seven?"

"Sounds about right." He smiled, a gentle but encouraging light in his eyes. The man didn't trust her to haul logs but he trusted her to sew up his body. Very strange. "You're doing great. Just do that a few more times."

She moved on to the second stitch, ignoring the warmth tickling her belly from his praise and his faith in her.

If this was a glimpse into what the coming month had for her, she wouldn't be bored.

But she should probably invest in a big bottle of aspirin.

Wyatt unlocked Amanda's back door and stepped into the mud room between the back porch and the kitchen. Amanda and her mother, Jolene, had twin cottages two hills down from the mountain. It was normal business for him to invade and use the shower whenever he pleased. Normal enough he'd forgotten to mention it to Imogen after she'd stitched his arm last night.

He didn't want to be impressed with the way she'd handled his little test. She had skills and, more importantly, she had the touch. Soothing. And at odds with the chemistry that roused urges in him he should ignore.

His thoughts had swung between irritated attraction and worry about how she would be with the patients. At best, she was someone they'd get used to and come to care about who'd quickly abandon them. Like all the times Josh had been passed from one transitory doctor to another. Sometimes they'd changed every visit. It kept things impersonal. A revolving door that left people not knowing who to trust. He didn't want that for his patients.

A few lights burned inside the cottage, enough that it looked like Imogen was awake, but when he knocked on the glass no one came. As tired as she'd been, there was a real chance she was still asleep, which would throw a wrench into their schedule. Wyatt waited another minute then let himself inside.

A quick check of the bedrooms assured him she was awake. The eventual sound of the shower told him where she was. He backtracked to the sofa and sat, mental images of her in the shower turning his thoughts back where he'd been fighting them since yesterday.

As pushy and stubborn as anyone he'd ever met, Wyatt couldn't put his finger on precisely what kept her in his mind—other than her appearance. He'd only really ever dated stereotypical South-ern women. Sweet, though sometimes he knew it to be an act. But not too challenging. Easy to understand, and because of that easy to be around. Easy on the eyes. Imogen may have that last bit, but there was nothing else easy about her. To be fair, she was a good nurse, so if she could handle the PR aspect of the position, she might be easy to work with.

The bathroom door opened and she came out, wrapped in a towel and swathed in billowing steam. Wyatt stared.

His presence caused her to gasp and clutch at the top of her towel, her hand folding over the place where one corner was tucked in, keeping it on. The action drew his gaze to her breasts, but the look on her face had him looking up again.

"You're here. What are you doing here?" She checked the front seam of her towel, making sure she was decently covered.

"No shower on the mountain yet."

When she didn't say anything else, he added, "I knocked. Then I used my key."

She frowned and nodded, turning toward the room she was sleeping in.

"Done in there?" Wyatt called after her.

"Yes." She stopped and looked from the bathroom to him. "The water. There's probably not much hot."

She hurt. He could tell by the way she moved, stiffly and slowly. She'd been trying to steam the soreness out of her body. It hadn't been a shower for cleanliness. Her hair was mostly dry, and secured in a fancy braid. Not a trace of the pink remained in the pale tresses. The baby-fine tendrils forming a halo around her clean face were damp and curling. A hot flush colored her skin, from the shower or her attire, he couldn't be sure. Not that he really cared. His body appreciated the result.

Wyatt cleared his throat. "It's fine. Be ready in half an hour."

He tried not to watch as she walked to the future nursery where she slept, wanting to see every inch on display and not wanting it at the same time. Guilt won and he dragged himself to the bathroom. She was in for a long day and it had already started on the wrong foot, sore from the logs he'd practically dared her to move.

The cold shower, surprisingly timely and bracing, sluiced over him with a wave of painful shivers. Wyatt placed both hands against the wall of the shower and stayed still until he could stand no more.

Any other day, he would've said the sight of an attractive woman wasn't enough to send his thoughts spiraling out of control. Any other day, he would've believed himself in control of his body.

It figured this would all happen on a week they were scheduled in towns with the dinkiest motels in history. He'd grown accustomed to sharing a double room with Amanda. It worked fine with cousins sharing; Amanda was as close as a sibling. As far as he could tell, the further along in her pregnancy she'd gotten, the more she liked having someone close by. But with Imogen...could that be a bad idea?

Nah. Well, probably not. They were adults. And after her first day deep in the mountains Wyatt doubted either of them would be feeling particularly lustful. Sometimes he felt almost as sensitive to the behavior and opinions of non-locals as his patients were, and he already knew what they'd think of Imogen. If only he'd managed to get a temp hired yesterday. The option of firing her spectacularly, distasteful as it was, might be just what had to happen.

"Imogen, we're almost there."

The voice, a low, manly rumble, distracted her

into wakefulness. And his scent… She'd thought she'd dreamed it. He smelled good, the whole front of the bus smelled like him. Her sleep-addled brain mixed with hormones surged in response to his extremely appealing pheromones. She didn't figure out what he'd said until she'd blinked away all that fog from her brain. "How long?"

"You've been asleep about two hours, and we're about half an hour out. We probably won't see as many patients today—the Trout Derby is on—but just in case, I want you prepared," Wyatt answered, while steering the big silver bus slowly down yet another winding country road—both doctor and driver of this practice on wheels. "I need to go over what's expected of you first, so wake up. Have some coffee." He handed her a thermos so she could refill her cup and drink herself sentient.

While she was waking up, he went through a list of common-sense expectations any nurse fresh out of school could have anticipated. Imogen only really felt awake when he got to the weird stuff.

"Wait… What?"

"Someone, probably an older lady, will come early and bring us something she made—food, usually baked goods of some description. Take some, even if it's just a little, and eat it. Thank her.

If you're feeling conversational, ask for the recipe. Be courteous, be nice, even if it seems weird. Most of our patients are children, who you probably can't offend, or the elderly who you can. Treat them like you would your grandparents."

"I never knew my grandparents, Wyatt, but I would never be rude to a patient." She really did need to wake up if she was going to maintain a professional attitude with him. All about family, right out of the gate. "And just so you know, I'm great with kids. And I don't run around hitting those of voting age with sticks and telling people they have ugly babies." Although after yesterday it might be unsurprising he thought the worst of her. She'd hoped her agreement to stitch him up would have negated their earlier interaction.

"Don't be dramatic. I'm not saying you're going to be rude, what I'm saying is that your definition of rude and the local definition will be different. Polite, distant professionalism is worse than rude here." He glanced at her long enough to establish eye contact and nodded once, then took his eyes back to the winding road.

"They want to treat us like family—and it won't be that way off the bat, but it's the goal. They'll listen to and respect care instructions if they think of you as family—someone here for the long haul. When they feel comfortable, they'll talk us up to their friends and families, and the number of patients will increase—which is crucial to getting the funding approved."

His dark eyes had been warmer yesterday, when he had been walking her through the stitches. Where had that guy gone? "Won't that kind of behavior from a stranger seem fake?"

"Not if you do it right. Try to be Amanda," Wyatt suggested, glancing her way again.

Message received. *You're not good enough.*

She could read between the lines. *Why can't you be like Amanda? My last nurse was better.*

My last girlfriend was prettier.

My last girlfriend knew how to make jam.

Imogen rubbed her head and drank more coffee. Coffee, good for more than waking you up. Also a great scapegoat to blame when your hands trembled.

Ignore it. He didn't think she could do the job. Fine. She had a month to prove him wrong. This judgmental stuff wasn't about her as a person.

He's not Scott.

The little mantras calmed her enough to get her hand under control, but Imogen still couldn't bring herself to look at him, knowing her eyes would be glassy and wet. Instead, she focused on the window. "Amanda is effusive with everyone." As the landscape rolled past, her vision cleared and her mind followed. "She'd take candy from a stranger then invite him home after announcing she lived alone and the nearest neighbor was a mile away."

"She's not that bad." Wyatt chuckled. Like any of this was funny. "But you had it right about the friendly-to-strangers bit. Not insanely trusting but friendly."

"I don't know how to be Southern and candy-sweet." Distance. Keep distance. Keep calm. He didn't know any better. His opinion didn't matter. Do the job. Go home. Pretend to drink the Kool-Aid, just don't swallow it.

"All I'm saying is be nice. Friendly. Think of something to say to personalize your interactions. Compliment patients, ask their advice, engage them somehow, and don't use any of your annoying tricks."

"Back to thinking I'll purposefully antagonize the patients? I have some training, you know." She took a deep breath, counted to ten and smiled past the lump in her throat. She could fake a smile. It was the least offensive mask she had, even if perhaps not the most healthy. "Anything else?"

Wyatt looked at her a little too long, but the road demanded his attention and, let off the hook, she looked back out the window.

"Two more things," Wyatt said. "One: there isn't much black and white out here—the law, and how stringently it's followed, is fluid. Don't get involved unless something is likely to harm the patient or someone else."

"Like?"

"I've treated and not reported a hunting accident before," Wyatt answered without hesitation, so matter-of-factly that he might have simply expressed his love of potatoes.

"A shooting?" That just seemed wrong. Dangerous.

"Shot himself in the leg, but missed any major trauma."

"That's..."

"Illegal. I know." He didn't seem fazed by it, though. "The patient was hunting in the off-season, which is to say: illegally. But the way I see it, and the way pretty much anyone in the area would see it, a man has a right to feed his family. Happened on his land. He's not well off, but he's making the most of what he has. I wouldn't want him punished for making sure his kids didn't go without."

"That's why you wanted me to stitch you up…" Imogen murmured, realization coming in a flash.

"That's why I wanted you to stitch me up."

"He could have lied about being the one to shoot him, you know." People lied all the time.

"I know, but he wasn't." Wyatt still seemed unfazed, and so sure of himself. Ego.

She nodded, still processing this information. The idea of putting her license on the line didn't appeal, but she could understand his logic. There was a certain kind of nobility to the decision, whether she would've made the same call or not. "At least it won't be boring."

"Last thing. If you have questions or concerns about one of my calls, make them in private—later, ideally. I need you to trust me and follow my orders without hesitation."

"I'll try," Imogen murmured, mostly because she wasn't ever sure exactly what she was going to do from moment to moment. And even if she'd never questioned a doctor's call in front of a patient before, she wasn't feeling too sure of anything. The job. Why she'd come. Him. Her worthiness as a nurse or a person. Amazing how fast all that could come rushing back. And she had thought she was past someone having the ability to make her feel so off. So small.

He turned the bus off the road and into a gravel lot beside a tiny white church, the kind quickie-wedding places and photographers liked to clone for ambiance.

"Do better than try." He sounded distant suddenly, and more than a little icy. Dr. Beechum had just arrived. A new mask came down, and Imogen didn't know which Wyatt was the real one—the one who walked her through stitches, the surly wild man on the mountain, or this icy man now walking to the back to start setting up.

Ditching her cup, she rubbed some warmth back into her suddenly chilled hands.

She hoped it was the last of his masks she'd have to watch out for.

She'd learned early on that when the masks came off, the monsters came out.

CHAPTER THREE

"EMMA-JEAN?" Like an immigrant to Ellis Island, Imogen had been renamed. And this time it wasn't a patient mangling her name.

The first couple of times she'd heard her name mispronounced by patients, Imogen had wanted to correct them. But in the spirit of following Wyatt's Grandpa Law she'd held back. That and because the patients seemed no more interested in talking to her than they might be to a wandering taxidermist who offered to kill and stuff their favorite pet for them.

Most of her smiles went unreturned. No one even wanted to talk about the fabulous weather, how green and lush everything was, how wonderful it smelled outside, with the honeysuckle blooming, or pretty much anything else she brought up.

Her efforts to find common ground with one older gentleman had even resulted in her being called a "damned do-gooder" for offering him a cup of coffee. Further alienating the patients wasn't high on her frustrating list of things to do. Coffee had been her go-to for common ground. Who didn't like coffee?

With a deep breath and after a few seconds to unclench her hands, Imogen turned to face Wyatt, who'd called her new name. He looked smug. He also looked like he needed someone to stomp on his toes. Someone like her. Later. After she played his stupid game.

"Yes, Doctor?"

"Next patient." He could've just said that, but that would have deprived him of the perverse pleasure he took in her predicament.

She stepped off the bus and made for the serene little church, today's waiting room, feeling not at all serene. Red carpet, wooden benches carved on the ends with crosses, an open stage in the front for the kind of preachers who needed room to wander. So quaint and peaceful it almost took the edge off her day. Her little oasis away from Wyatt.

Inside, a handful of people sat—most of whom had spent the day there, chatting while people came and went from the bus. She snagged the sign-in sheet from the table beside the door and called the last name on the check-in sheet. "Mr. Smith?"

Day almost over. Just one more patient.

An older man stood with some effort and as he turned to look back, ice lanced through her middle. *Blue skin.*

Oh, no. His skin tone rivaled a blueberry, bluer than anyone she'd ever seen. She'd coded patients in her time, she just hadn't expected it to happen on this job.

Fear, bright and blistering, sent her running for the man. "Sir, it's going to be okay. Sit back down. Breathe for me. Sit. Yes." She urged him back onto the wooden pew, ready to throw him on his back to give CPR.

Assess. Breathing somewhat labored, but he still breathed. He looked a little alarmed but not panicky. Didn't exactly add up. She needed Wyatt. Blue skin was a bad sign. "Someone get Dr. Beechum."

Everyone in the room stared at her, shock and horror on their faces—and not one of them equipped to run for Wyatt.

With the man seated, she confirmed his pulse was more or less regular then held up one hand to signal he should stay, and barreled for the bus. The door had barely opened before she started shouting, "Wyatt! A patient inside is cyanotic. I think he's coding…"

Wyatt grabbed a tank of oxygen and a mask, and ran behind her.

She was nearly at Mr. Smith's side when Wyatt took her by the elbow and thrust her behind him. "Oh, sir, I'm so sorry. My nurse is new—Emma-Jean, Amanda's friend. Don't think she's ever encountered anyone with methoglobinemia before."

Her breathing sounded so loud in her ears Imogen couldn't even be sure she understood what Wyatt was saying. The man wasn't coding? Blue skin happened when someone was deprived of oxygen. Blue skin was never good.

The two men exchanged a few quiet words and the next thing she knew, Wyatt was peddling her backwards, out of earshot, his big body blocking her view of the bizarrely colorful man. "Take a walk, Emma-Jean."

"Please tell me what's going on. That man—"

"He's descended from the Blue Fugates of Troublesome Creek." Wyatt leaned close as he spoke, like she knew the people or the creek. It was a hell of a time for him to invade her space and fill her nose with his good smell. It just got warmer and fuller the longer the day wore on. And with her adrenaline surging, her senses only multiplied her reaction to it.

"Take your phone, walk up the hill and run a search on it. Come back in a half hour, I'll explain if needed."

"I'm sorry. I thought…"

"I know." His voice gentled but he still looked grim. "You're embarrassed, and so is he. Take a walk."

Imogen nodded, and though she wanted to apologize to the man for causing a scene, she slipped to the exit with as much dignity as she could muster.

She felt the burning in her eyes before she got to the door but managed to hold back a well of frustrated tears—they got no further than her lashes. Horrified didn't begin to cut it.

Shaking started deep in her shoulders, aftereffects of adrenaline. A simple walk up the hill wouldn't suffice. She had to move.

Once clear of the building, Imogen broke into a jog. For a few minutes the scorching embarrassment from nearly coding poor Mr. Smith deadened the soreness that had racked her body since yesterday.

Wyatt's repeated warnings that she wouldn't fit in had sounded like a bunch of excuses before today. All her efforts to engage the patients, all the resisting of correcting the pronunciation of her name, all her good work…gone, in the wake of one well-intentioned mistake.

It figured that he'd be right about her fitting in but wrong about her having cell reception at the top of the hill. No bars again. The mountains rejected both her and her cellphone. What was she even doing here?

The surge of energy left as quickly as it had arrived, and rather than walk back down to the bus and chance an encounter with the blue grandpa, she hopped over the ditch on the shoulder of the road, walked into the trees and sat.

Day One—Epic Failure. Would he even allow her to attempt Day Two? Should she count herself lucky if he went ahead and fired her spectacularly later?

When Mr. Smith had been gone for twenty minutes and Imogen still hadn't returned, Wyatt stored any loose items and started the bus. Not the greatest day on record, but at least she hadn't started chest compressions and broken Mr. Smith's sternum.

Wyatt considered the thought and dismissed it. Imogen might be a little culturally clueless for the region, but she was a good nurse. When the situation had failed to compute for her, she had come for him. It had been the right call.

He found her sitting beside the road, right where he'd told her to go, knees up and hand to forehead, propping it up. With little enough traffic on the country road, he stopped. A few seconds later he heard the bus door open and close, and finally she joined him.

"You all right?" Wyatt asked, not starting the bus again yet—no one waited behind them and he wanted to look at her. No anger, though the set of her shoulders and her refusal to look at him said enough. Dismay. Disappointment. Maybe even defeat.

"I'm fine. Can we go?"

She wasn't fine, but was obviously not ready to talk about it. When they reached the motel and had settled in, he'd try again.

She buckled in and he got the bus moving, letting her soak up some peace as they made the forty-five-minute drive to the nearest little town and the motel he usually stayed at.

Family-owned motels were what Wyatt preferred. They were tiny, but they were also friendly, not connected to the interstate so they felt safer, and the owners happily learned his route and saved a room for him. The colors the rooms sported had probably been hideous even when new, but for some reason their homeliness tickled him. Something he appreciated after years of a cosmopolitan lifestyle. They were also extremely clean. Another selling point.

Pulling off into the gravel lot of his usual stop, Wyatt realized two things: no Wi-Fi, so he was going to have to get Imogen to talk at least enough to explain what happened with Mr. Smith; and the Trout Derby might have filled his usual room. Ten rooms in the whole building, and by his count there were ten vehicles in the lot.

Shutting off the ignition, he climbed out of his seat and headed for the door. "Wait here. I'll make sure they still have the room waiting."

Imogen had given no indication she intended to move, but he said it anyway.

"Okay."

One-word answers from the talkative woman... From the number of cars, if they had a room saved, it was going to be just that: one room, which was what they always saved.

Imogen watched Wyatt cross the lot and enter the office before it dawned on her that he'd said *"a room.*" Singular. One. Did he intend on staying in the bus?

She should stop him before he spent money on the wrong accommodations. Moving quickly was off the menu for the foreseeable future—her body ached more than ever after sitting still for so long—but with a cup of effort and a bushel of unladylike noises, she peeled herself off the seat and made her way off the bus.

Wyatt stood at the counter, talking and laughing with the rosy-cheeked, grandmotherly innkeeper, charm personified. Another new mask. Were they gossiping? He had never once tried to charm her. Because he didn't want her working for him. And maybe he also just didn't like her. She didn't rate Charm Face. Well, she didn't particularly like him either, so whatever.

"Dr. Beechum." Screw him and his renaming her. She'd still say his name however he wanted—regardless of the spelling. It was called being a professional. "Pardon me, did you say *a* room?"

When he turned to look at her, the smile left his deep brown eyes. "Yes, and Miss Arlene has saved the room for us."

"To share?"

"Double room."

"To *share*?" she repeated, leaning heavily on the second word to drill its importance into him. Why couldn't she have promised Amanda that she'd just come and take care of her, not her job? Then she wouldn't be stuck about to share a room with a man who...who...who...was bossy. And stuff.

"Amanda never minded." He cleared his throat, smiled at Arlene and leaned away from the counter to approach Imogen.

"You're her cousin! She has to like you well enough to share a room. And she's Amanda. Even if she minded, she wouldn't mind." Why was she yelling? Imogen stopped the flow of words and rubbed the tension from her forehead. Maybe she'd just sleep on the bus. There weren't any blankets, but there were pain relievers and really uncomfortable vinyl exam tables.

Sigh. Too tired. Way too sore.

"She had a long day and dragged felled timber for me yesterday," Wyatt said to Arlene, making more excuses for her behavior. This day just kept getting better.

"Come on." Key in hand, he winked at Arlene and then steered Imogen out of the office and to the nearby room. "Run a bath and soak, it'll help. I'll put your bag outside the door and fetch dinner."

"There aren't any other rooms available, are there." She couldn't manage more than the faintest trace of a question in her tone, just giving the realization a voice.

"Not for about thirty miles." He paused inside the room, hand on the knob, ready to exit again. "Want to go there?"

Imogen looked around the room, the full weight of the décor hitting her at once. "Do they film porn in here?"

Wyatt made a sound like a laugh he'd barely stopped.

"Oh, man, they do. And now I've got that music in my head." Imogen sighed. "But with banjos."

"Banjo porn soundtracks," Wyatt said with a chuckle. "There's probably a kink for that. The orange carpet and green refrigerator may be a little loud, but it's impeccably clean." He left his hand on the knob, ready to open the door again. "Want to go?"

It meant something that he would offer. Thirty more miles or a bath now?

Who was she kidding?

"It's fine." Not really, but they were both adults—in theory—and she wasn't in the mood to care. She was in the mood to pamper her aching body, and that meant hot water and silence. She grabbed a towel and stepped into the bathroom, shutting the door and locking it.

Let him go do whatever he wanted, fetch whatever he wanted, apologize for her rude bathing and door-locking ways to whomever he happened to stumble across.

As she sank into the hot water, she began to feel a little more reasonable. Everything would be okay. Except for the part where they'd be sharing a room.

No. She could do this. She'd hauled his logs. She'd illegally stitched his arm. She could spend a night sleeping a short distance from the man she'd found so attractive *before* today.

His proximity, by turns, gave her both intensely naughty visuals and made her want to punch him where it counted. But it could be there was some happy place in between where she could merely tolerate his existence without strong feelings one way or the other.

So long as he didn't go shirtless. She didn't like him shirtless. Well, she did, but it could be a problem. Or maybe seeing him parade around shirtless would warm her to him enough to make it through tomorrow.

Just as she thought about toweling off, he

knocked on the door and called through it, "Got dinner. It's still hot." Implied command: get out here and eat. Too tired and hungry to make a fuss, she called her assent and climbed out of the tub. The water was growing cold anyway.

As promised, her bag sat outside the door and she dragged it inside.

Normally, she'd just pull on her robe and let it dry her. But could she do that with him out there? No. Now she had to move her sore body to dry herself and then put on pajamas, and all she had was pink and strappy and covered in garish red kiss marks.

She put the robe over it. Let him stay curious about her anatomy until he deserved to see it.

When she got herself together enough to exit the bathroom, she found him standing by the door, takeout set out on the table, complete with paper napkins, plastic utensils, and water poured into actual glasses from a tall, cold bottle.

"Didn't know what you like. The Trout Derby's on and there's a lady who sets up a fish shack. Fried, with grilled potatoes, mixed vegetables." He looked uncomfortable too. *Good.*

Maybe she should take off her robe just to increase his discomfort. Level the playing field. Or not. The air-conditioning was cold…

"Thanks." She pulled the towel off her head and took a minute to comb her hair out before sitting down. He waited, for some reason.

"About earlier," he began, taking his seat opposite her at the small table. "It's called methemoglobinemia. Overproduction of methemoglobin. I'll spare you the details, but he's been blue since birth and while it's rarer now than, say…sixty or seventy years ago, there's a stigma and a kind of urban legend that goes along with it around here."

She nodded for him to continue, making a mental note to read more about it when they were somewhere with an internet connection. "And that legend is?"

"That it's caused by inbreeding."

"Oh, no." The full weight of Mr. Smith's condition began to penetrate and with it went Imogen's appetite. The fish had looked good just a few seconds ago. School must have been hell for Mr. Smith. Living in the area must still be hell for him.

"It's not, by the way. A family settled here a couple of centuries ago, up Troublesome Creek, had a bunch of kids. All at least carriers of the gene,"

Wyatt said, effectively drawing her attention from her personal mortification to professional curiosity.

"So the creek didn't make him blue?"

"No. Both parents have to pass the gene on, so it's exceptionally rare. But with that large number of carriers at the start of the community, by the time you fast-forward a hundred and fifty years, loads of people in the area carry the gene. And sometimes two marry, and a child turns up blue," Wyatt explained, holding off on his dinner while he talked. "It's a sensitive subject to those affected."

"And I really stepped in it with poor Mr. Smith."

Wyatt winced and leaned back. "You made an honest mistake."

The wince bought him some points. "Why did you make me leave?"

"I was just trying to kill the subject fast." He lifted both hands, like he was afraid she was going to start shouting at him again. "I wasn't trying to punish you."

"It seemed…"

"I know," he said, and after a second admitted, "Didn't figure that out until you didn't come back."

"There's no cure for him?"

"No cure. There's treatment. Some treat it, some don't. It's high maintenance—leaves the system fast. Not everyone is as blue as Mr. Smith, some are just tinged." Right now he seemed far removed from the man she'd spent two days angry with. This was a good mask. Almost a friend mask. "I'm sorry. I didn't think to warn you about it before we went. I don't see him that often, it just didn't even occur to me."

Imogen drew a deep breath, surprised at the apology. He hadn't set her up, and that was something small to cling to in the travesty of a day.

The fish really did look good, covered in cornmeal and curling from the deep fry. She took a bite and grinned at him.

"You might not be thrilled with the accommodations but there are perks. The food's good. And the views…especially come autumn." Okay, maybe he had saved some charm for her. He really had a nice smile. When he used it.

"No denying that the food is good," Imogen murmured, and, unable to help it, added, "Or the view. I might have to invite myself back to the mountain to see the foliage from the ridge. You know, since you might fire me spectacularly before then."

Wyatt leaned back in his chair, those dark eyes pinning her to her seat. Was he about to fire her spectacularly?

"Do you want me to fire you?" He might be considering it. Or maybe he just wanted to keep that option in reserve for when she wasn't expecting it. Biggest impact then…

"Are you going to fire me if I say no?" Imogen asked, steadily holding his gaze. Great eyes. Dark. Almost black…

"No."

She didn't know whether that was good news or bad news, so she pushed past it. "I don't run from things that are *hard.*"

"What do you run from?"

Relationships. Jobs. Houses. Commitments. People. Not precisely right, but not really wrong either. Her exes had called her fickle for a reason, but past that first mistake she'd always been upfront about the fact that she'd never stay.

"Nothing," she said. "Why did you ask that?"

"You emphasized 'hard,' not 'run.'"

"I didn't." Imogen squinted, shaking her head.

"You definitely did." Wyatt kept watching her in that way that made her want to leave the room. "And someone who lives on the road…"

"Monotony," she blurted out. Monotony, monogamy—whatever.

"You run from monotony?" Wyatt asked, his brows lifted like he didn't believe her.

"Yes." True. Ish. Truer than any other way she could put into words.

"Then you should enjoy this position. Never a dull moment." He didn't call her on it, and even tried to make her smile again. "Except for those moments when nothing happens."

"Does it always involve living together?" No smiling through that part. Living together was bad. Bad, and worse, and nothing good could come from it.

"Would it make you feel better about the accommodations if I promised not to banish you from the site again?"

"No." She shuffled the food around in the container, trying to silence the little inner voice that shouted she was being unreasonable. "My roommate track record isn't good. Even in college, as much as I love her, it was hard to live with Amanda. I need space and quiet."

"Fair enough." He reached for his water. "For tonight I can give you quiet and we'll try for separate rooms from here on out. Deal?"

"Deal." Peace and quiet was what she needed. She didn't need him charming her like he did the innkeeper. Imogen went back to the fish, feeling better, all things considered. "He was really blue. And all that white facial hair! I bet you anything people torment that poor man with Smurf jokes. Might even be preferable to the urban legend jokes."

Wyatt chuckled and threw a closed salt packet at her, bouncing it off her chin. "No making fun of the patients."

"I'm serious. I feel bad for him. And I just feel bad about it in general." What had brought on the sudden confession? That needed to stop. She threw the salt pack back at him.

He caught it and grinned at her. "Have to do better than that."

"I don't have to do anything. You're not the boss of me," Imogen sassed, trying to get past the emotion.

"Am too." Wyatt tossed the packet in the trash and began tidying up.

Imogen let him have the last word.

And pretended his smile didn't warm her.

Almost dark.

When the lights went off, she would be safe. Wyatt would go to sleep and stop moving around, drawing attention to himself. And he'd be under the covers, transforming himself into a quilt-covered lump and stop drawing attention to himself by lying there, all…big for the bed. Tall. Big. She liked a big man.

Wyatt would be good with his hands. And his mouth. Heck, he could probably make banjo porn music sexy. How would he react to that suggestion? The man had so many masks he still might have a Psychotic Nutjob Face in reserve. That would make working together impossible.

A fling with Dinner Face? Imogen could get used to that idea. Forget the day's stress. Forget the length of her Appalachian prison sentence.

She closed her eyes and laid her head back against the headboard where she sat—stiff, sore and surly. It didn't matter what he did, he disrupted her peace and quiet. Closing her eyes made her other senses go supersonic.

In trying not to look at him, it became impossible not to hear his every move. Worse, his bed lay between hers and the air-conditioning unit, so it constantly blew Eau de Mountain Man in her direction. He smelled good. Really good! The kind of good that kept making her sneak looks at him.

The attraction was too strong, and Imogen knew

the limits of her endurance. At some point, unless he trotted out his Psychotic Nutjob, she was going to make a pass.

But not tonight.

With a sigh, she dragged herself out of the bed and marched to her bag to dig out her perfume. She doused her pulse points, and ended with a swipe of her perfume-dampened wrist beneath her nose. That should do the trick. Ruggedly manly man scent could never get past her favorite fragrance. Not even the scent of the large, stupidly attractive and rugged manly man disrupting her peace and quiet.

"Do I stink?" Wyatt asked, alerting her to the fact that he was watching her act like a crazy woman over the top edge of his computer tablet.

Yes. She wanted to say yes, but that wouldn't be nice and he was trying to keep his word to give her quiet. "No." She put her perfume back and thought up a lie to cover her insanity. "The fish. I smell the fish."

"Right." He put his tablet down, stood and a minute later was out the door with the remains of dinner.

Imogen took the opportunity to rid herself of her robe and climb into bed. She was under the covers with her back to him when he returned, but she still couldn't relax. More so now. Lying down seemed to amplify the soreness racking her body. The simple act of relaxing the muscles made sneaky pained sounds escape her.

Wyatt returned to find Imogen in bed. Between today, yesterday's log moving and however long she'd driven before that, he couldn't blame her for getting to bed early. He was even a little grateful.

As quietly as he could, he locked the door, shut the curtains and turned out every light but one—he had a little work to finish before turning in. One of the perks of a small practice was not as much paperwork and file maintenance required as there would be when the practice grew, but he needed meticulous files as backup for the funding application.

Imogen rolled over from her side onto her belly, and made a little sound. Pain. He looked back over at her, squirming under the blanket.

"Want some painkillers?"

"I'm okay."

Liar.

Wyatt watched her settle for about thirty seconds

and then shift again, clearly looking for a comfortable position. "Are you going to do that all night?"

"Bath is wearing off," she mumbled, sounding miserable.

"Back?"

"Shoulders, arms, back, butt, legs. Pretty much *everything* hurts."

He could help that. "Right." He put the tablet aside and stepped over to the bed, grabbing the quilt and pushing it down to her waist as he sat.

"What are you doing?" she asked, and looked at him accusingly. "How come you're not hurting after falling down and getting cut up?"

"Be still. I'm helping." He put a hand to the center of her back and pushed her down on the bed. "I'm a tough hillbilly. They start rolling us down the hills to toughen us up when we're babies."

"I don't want your help." She paused and then added, "Or your silly stories."

"I know this grouchiness is the way you charm men, but shut up, Imogen." He flattened his hand between her shoulder blades and pressed again, willing her to listen even if he had grave doubts she'd ever stop being contrary. "Be still. You are certainly the most stubborn woman I've ever met."

And that shouldn't tickle him, but for some reason it made him want to rile her.

She stopped trying to sit up and actually went silent. Amazing.

She's just like a patient. Wyatt tried to ignore the feel of her skin under his hands as he kneaded her shoulders, which were knotted from exertion but stiff from something else—wariness, maybe? After a couple of minutes' insistent kneading, she started to relax. The nightclothes she wore blocked his access so he said, "I need your top off. You stay facedown. I'm not looking for a cheap thrill here."

She was quiet a few seconds and he waited. Her nod was brief, uncertain, but pain often trumped caution. He pushed the garment to her ribs and waited for her to lift and pull the material past her breasts so he could get it off her arms and back to work.

It was just a shirt. Nothing erotic about helping a patient remove restrictive clothing...

CHAPTER FOUR

WHEN IMOGEN SETTLED back down on the bed, Wyatt got to work. God, she was soft. Her muscles might currently feel like rocks under her skin, but that skin was soft. He moved down her back, his thumbs working the muscles along both sides of her spine.

What began as kindness took on completely different feeling as the soft sounds she made went from pain to pleasure. She wasn't shy with the sounds either. Wyatt realized his breathing had increased. His mouth was dry.

He wanted this infuriating, stubborn woman. He also genuinely wanted to make her feel better.

There was one certain way to make her relax, but seeing that he'd forced this single-room accommodation on her, it seemed sort of scummy to make the pass he wanted to. Honor wouldn't let him. Wouldn't let him press his lips to the back of her neck or explore the soft contours of her body. Really wouldn't let him strip down and join her.

He swallowed, concentrating on the muscle he kneaded, not on the way she stretched and shifted like a cat beneath his touch.

"That feels really good." Her voice was muffled, but he heard every word, felt every breath.

Supple. She grew softer as the tortured muscles began to soften beneath his touch.

More real than a fantasy, Wyatt could almost feel the soft scrape of his tongue on her satiny skin, gliding down along each little dip along her spine, feel the muscles he worked so hard to soften tense up again as she arched against him.

"I like you better like this," Imogen murmured.

Talking. Talking would save him. "Like what?" He cleared his throat and tried to focus. Focus. And stop panting like a dog.

"Nice…and attentive."

Attentive. She had all his damned attention. The blankets were in his way and he pushed them roughly to the side and followed her spine down to the dimples on either side, just above the waist of her ridiculous pink shorts. He'd always gone for women who knew all of Victoria's Secrets, silk and lace being the least of them, but these snug cotton shorts squeezed the round cheeks up in a way that demanded discovery. Demanded he get the material out of the way and sink his teeth into the plump little curve that blended butt to thigh.

"When you're working you're kind of an ass."

Ass. Yes. Wait. Again? "I heard that somewhere recently."

She laughed a little and he found himself grinning despite the insult. "Sorry."

"I don't think I've ever been called an ass by a patient before."

"I'm not a patient. I'm your..." Imogen laughed again and then waved a hand weakly. "Nothing. Never mind."

"No, you have to say it now." Being called an ass should cool his libido. Any second now. He dragged his gaze away from her ass and went to work on the back of one thigh, squeezing and releasing the tense muscle. This wasn't any smarter.

"It's bad. Bad Imogen. Emma-Jean. I'm trying... practice...impulse control."

"Me too."

"You have impulse-control problems?" She yawned, more than half-asleep already.

"Yes." Maybe it was contagious. He'd never really had them before. "Now shut up and go to sleep."

"Can't sleep with your big man hands on me." Imogen mumbled.

Wyatt sat back, tilting his head to try and get a look at her face, which was mostly hidden between her arms, the pillow, and the thick braid she'd worked it into while wet. "Feeling better?"

"Mmm-hmm. Thank you. Now go away."

Right. Go away. Don't climb between her legs and take her from behind. "Good night." He pulled the covers back over her so she didn't have to move, and got up.

Massaging her hadn't been curative, it had just run her tension through some supercharging system and transferred it to his body.

After a pause to turn off the last light, he grabbed his bag and headed for the shower. Cold shower. His second today. All his good intentions to keep his distance had already almost completely abandoned him by the end of Day One. And he hadn't even kissed her yet.

Sleep wouldn't come easily tonight.

Imogen felt a big hand pet her head, warm and gentle, pushing the baby hairs back from her face as the low, manly voice rumbled her name.

Nice. He said her name again and she smiled, for once not bothered to be pulled from sleep.

When she opened her eyes, no one was there,

but Wyatt stood at the other end of the bed, fully clothed and ready for the day, jostling her mattress with his leg as he said her name. "Time to get up."

"Were you over here a minute ago?" *Petting my head like a lover.*

"No. I'm going to get started."

So he hadn't just been there, caressing her from a deep slumber. And he looked ticked off about something already. Was his doctor mask in place so soon?

He had even packed already, and he stopped to grab his bag on the way to the door. "Need to leave in an hour. Room's yours."

"Okay. I'll be ready. Just gotta wake up." Remembering her missing top, she stayed under the blankets until he was out of the room, then grabbed her robe and made a dash for the bathroom.

He'd been so sweet last night. Maybe he wasn't a morning person. Maybe his better qualities were tied to the moon—reverse werewolf-style. Now that the sun was up, he was back to being an idiot.

Deciding it would be better to make it to the bus earlier rather than later, she washed, brushed, clothed herself and packed in record time. Half an hour later she was on the bus, still a bit bleary-eyed and looking for coffee. With Wyatt off in one of the two exam rooms, she took her time over her travel mug, doctoring the strong brew with cream and extra sugar. It was an extra-sugar morning, said her nerves.

Mornings had always been the hardest with Scott. He'd got up earlier than she had for cow-milking duty and had had no patience for her sleepiness when he'd finally stroll in around six a.m., wanting breakfast after already having worked two hours. She'd learned to wake up fast and it had become ingrained.

Not that her relationship with Scott was anything like this situation. She and Wyatt weren't together, it was just some weird hangover from having to sleep in the same room last night.

"How are you feeling today?" he asked from the doorway.

"Good." At least physically. "Much better than the past couple days. I realize I owe that to you, so thank you."

He stopped beside her, his expression troubled. "We need to talk."

She snapped the lid on her coffee and put the cup down so she could give him her undivided attention. It felt heavy, whatever he was about to say, and she tried to think of what she had said to him the night before. She could have stepped in it again and not remember. Was he grinding his teeth?

Seconds ticked by, butterflies twisting her insides as she watched him mentally wrestle with something and say nothing.

"Wyatt, what is it?"

The next she knew, he was against her, his mouth burning hot and rough against hers. Not the way she'd imagined their first kiss. Caught so off guard, she could do little more than react instinctively. Her arms came up under his as he steered her backwards to the wall and ground her against it, kissing with the length of his big body.

She'd always liked kissing—good, wholesome fun, kissing. This was nothing like the playful, gentle kisses she'd found on the lips of any other men. It overwhelmed her, burning away every other thought, claiming every part of her—a flow of something hot and molten that dragged her down, burning her lips, singeing her tongue, searing her from the inside out with his breath that she breathed.

When he lifted his head, she could only stare at him, light-headed and shaking, her arms still locked around his shoulders. Broad, warm, and steady…and she couldn't think of anything but kissing him again.

Imogen tried to get control of her breathing, but continued to hold onto him lest he get any ideas about letting go before she got her balance. Say something. Quick! "I like the way you talk." That was what came out, followed by a bubble of semi-nervous giggles.

Smooth.

His gaze fell heavy on hers. Dark. Troubled. Although the giggles ceased, words still failed to materialize—and she was usually so good at talking.

"We need to go," he said a heartbeat before she gave in to the impulse to kiss him again. "Get your coffee and get into your seat."

Damn. She had been going to make that pass at him, regardless of the mask situation. But he stepped around her like she was a bump in the road and headed for the driver's seat. Like this was just how he liked to start his day. Another tick on the itinerary. Kiss Nurse: check.

"No walking around while the bus is in motion." Imogen mumbled one of yesterday's rules beneath her breath, the only words that came to the vacuum that had become her mind. She'd hold off on that pass until the day was over. No doubt by the end of the day she'd be too traumatized again to think of jumping him.

Her hands shook as she finished locking down the coffee station and took her seat. He started the engine and ignored her. The only proof she had that he knew she was even there came in the tension of his shoulders and the fierce scowl she'd not seen since she'd stormed his mountain and interrupted his chainsawing.

Imogen fastened her seat belt and turned her attention away from him to the window. Feeling put out, she muttered, "Glad we got that sorted out."

Wyatt went through a checklist with his current patient and tried to get Imogen off his mind. Luckily for him, most patients on this stop were in maintenance mode—not many new ailments, stable medication roster—nothing that required much brain power.

He'd told her they needed to talk and had then thrust his tongue into her mouth like some gawky kid trying to tell the prettiest girl in school that he liked her. He took one comfort in the knowledge that he hadn't resorted to pulling her hair and running away.

He hadn't run at all. It had been more like a brisk, purposeful walk to the driver's seat.

No doubt she'd picked out a few choice names for him, at least if the way she stared at him meant anything. He swung between thinking she'd yell and thinking she might punch him in the junk at any moment. Whatever fate he faced, it would have to wait until the end of the day. God help him if she failed to control those impulses of hers in front of patients.

After seeing his last patient out, Wyatt noted that Exam Two was empty. He found Imogen in the front, waiting for him. Alone. "Next patient?"

"No one else until after lunch," she said matter-of-factly, leaning one hip against the coffee counter and crossing her arms over her chest.

"I'm not hungry."

"Liar." She snorted at him and moved away from the counter to prowl closer. Here it came. He should be glad she'd waited until the patients were out of earshot. "You are hungry, and even if you weren't, it wouldn't matter." A grin suddenly tickled the corners of her mouth and she fought to keep a straight face. "Your patients all brought covered dishes, Doctor." With that, she lost her battle with the laugh she'd been holding in.

Could he blame her for laughing? This was a new one for him too. Had they done this kind of thing when he'd been a kid? "Why…?"

"Well, according to Miss Dottie, since you always come on the day before their monthly Grange meeting, they decided to start having it on Tuesday instead of Wednesday to keep from spending two days in a row here."

"Won't we be crashing the meeting if we go?" Wyatt stepped to the door and looked out the window. The doors of the old converted single-room schoolhouse stood open and inside were long tables either piled with foil-covered dishes or lined with people in chairs, waiting.

"I asked that too," Imogen said, seeming to forget she had been angry with him in favor of this strange situation. "None of them are farmers anymore so they don't really have Grange business to deal with. But they like getting together to eat, play games and listen to music so much that they still pay their Grange dues and keep the charter. I think it's kind of a tradition for people to be in the farmers' organization here. Their parents and grandparents and yadda-yadda…"

She paused, considered something and shrugged. "Or maybe it's just better to have an official club to go to, otherwise you'd have to call it the monthly party. Monthly meeting sounds much less frivolous."

"Music too?" Wyatt cleared his throat, frowning to hint that she needed to sober up. It was very strange, but laughing at the locals would definitely make the patients not think of them as family—something he still had trouble picturing, even though he knew it was the right goal.

"Not just any music. Foot-stompin' music." She giggled again, and he prayed she got it out of her system before they went inside. "After we eat. They're waiting on us. Better go if you want your patients to love you and tell their friends. This is your big chance."

He turned toward the door, but she grabbed his arm. Contact with her flesh sent a shock through him. Before he could think of anything to say, she stepped in and in low tones that reminded him she still harbored some anger muttered, "That means be charming. Follow your own advice, Doctor, and Be Nice. Don't be the ass you've been again all day."

She released his hand and stepped past him, leaving him to follow.

Well, that could have gone much worse.

* * *

In any normal week Imogen would've been horrified by the amount of calories she'd consumed in the past twenty-four hours. She told herself it was okay, she'd built up some kind of calorie allowance by playing pack mule for Wyatt and then hiking up a mountain on Sunday.

Moderation prevailed, part of her impulse-control program, and she took a page from Wyatt's Big Book of Coping Mechanisms, and refused to even look at the dessert table. Just like he'd refused to look at the bus and now refused to look at her. She should break into it the next time he was off with his chainsaw, see what the big deal was.

Somehow while not looking at her, he managed to make her feel watched. He kept an open chair beside him, an invitation for her to sit, but it didn't take a neurosurgeon to figure out why: he didn't trust her around the patients. She needed space. At least, until she figured out what the kiss had meant.

Imogen made her way to an empty section of table and sat, risking possible outsider rudeness in distancing herself from everyone, but she needed distance. Her nerves needed some time to relax. She might accidentally try to code someone again who didn't actually need it.

Her sentence was six months, and although that extended time frame might make it hard to keep her required distance, it wasn't a lifetime. It might even make things better between them if she made the second move and just invited him to put his hands anywhere on her he liked. A tension breaker could solve some of this. Besides, his hands were nice. Not soft, like most doctors' hands. Not rough either, but they had a kind of crispness that intrigued her. Felt more real somehow.

Tension breaker. One night on offer. He could show her how mountain men did things, then she'd go to her own room and tomorrow there wouldn't be this tension between them. A short-term fling, maybe even one night. And maybe someone to help with his cabin if it didn't require hauling logs. She liked it there in the woods, and seeing the cabin going up thrilled her for some inexplicable reason. Probably something in the air.

A squeaking sound beside her announced the arrival of a couple of older ladies. Imogen smiled at them both, unsure what to say. One of them carried a bag of yarn and she proceeded to drag it out and start working on some project as they took turns pumping Imogen for information.

Where was she from? Who were her people?

How did she like the area? With them supplying the topic, and Imogen on her best behavior, it wasn't so bad. When a lull in the conversation came around, she panicked and the first words out of her mouth were a lie. "Wyatt's looking for someone to make a baby blanket for Amanda's baby." He wasn't. He probably hadn't thought anything about gifts for the baby.

Imogen had already made her baby gift purchase: a crib, which should come in the mail some time soon and which she would put together. She could do it. Handy and all that.

Wyatt's constant monitoring and her first disastrous day on the job had made her a little paranoid. She waited for the woman, Divina, to say something. It took a few seconds' hard thinking then she smiled and they went with the new topic. The best yarns for babies. The best stitches to use. How about a cap and booties? Sure!

Smiling and talking about babies offended people less frequently than accidentally trying to code them.

They talked long past the time she should've gone back to work, and by the end of the conversation she'd somehow ordered a complete set of hand-made baby stuff for Wyatt to give for the baby. And later she'd have to tell him he was buying it. Not awkward at all. She got a contact number and excused herself, feeling stuck somewhere between weirded out and proud that she'd managed to juggle conversation dynamite for a whole hour without offending anyone.

And they liked her. They welcomed her. They even seemed to like her better once she started them talking about something personal to her. And all without fake compliments and sugary Southern sweetness. She'd never needed it anywhere else she'd lived. Why had she let him put her on edge? People picked up on that kind of thing. Probably had something to do with how things had gone yesterday. Up until she'd tried to code poor Mr. Smith.

She found Wyatt outside with some of the older men, one of whom they'd seen earlier that day: Mr. Shoemaker.

They were playing horseshoes. Maybe he had listened to her advice after all.

Or maybe he hadn't. There was not a smile to be found among them, and Wyatt chewed on nothing—like he did when he was brooding. She didn't know exactly what they were talking about, but the tension in his tall frame rivaled what she'd felt yesterday.

"I just mean that we're real glad you come home again, boy. It weren't right for your daddy to put all that on you, like he done," Mr. Shoemaker said as Wyatt released a horseshoe with far too much strength. It soared several feet past the pole. "It's a pity you two couldn't work it out before he passed."

"Yes, sir," Wyatt managed, straightening up. "Glad to be home too." He caught sight of Imogen across the yard and nodded. "You ready to get back to work, Emma-Jean?" Neither of them made a pretext of using her real name today.

"Yes, Doctor." She smiled at the men then added, "I was just about to ask you the same question." Today he was the one who needed rescuing. Funny how that had happened.

Wyatt broke away from the group after shaking hands with everyone, but Imogen felt compelled somehow to smooth things over with these men she didn't know. With Wyatt out of earshot, it couldn't violate her rules about keeping distance to comment, "Not sure I'll be any use to him. Think I ate my weight in the green beans and corn bread. I heard someone say that the music was going to start any minute, so I'm sure we'll be back out here to listen as soon as we're done seeing patients. Grateful for you all inviting us. Best meal in forever."

"We'll look for you again next month," one of the men said.

And Mr. Shoemaker approached her and laid a hand on her arm as he murmured to her, "You keep an eye on him, Emma-Jean. He's had a lot on him."

"Yes, sir," Imogen replied, not sure what else to say. He looked so worried she had to ask, "You were friends with his father?"

"Not for more than twenty years, but we used to run together when we was young. After the boy died, his daddy stopped talking to 'most anybody."

"Oh." Boy died. He must mean the brother, but she'd thought that the mother and brother had died at the same time, like in a crash or something. And if his dad had put all that on Wyatt... She looked back toward the bus and then again into the pale, concerned eyes of the older man.

This was exactly the kind of situation she didn't like to deal with. Too raw. Too easy to hurt someone when they were already hurt. Not just Wyatt. This man looked hurt by whatever had happened. It was too much for her to work out the right words so she gave in to impulse and hugged him, kissed his cheek and then jogged back to the bus.

"Hey," Imogen said as she stepped into the bus and closed the door. "Are you okay?"

"Yeah, I'm okay." He didn't sound okay.

Imogen stepped over to him but was careful to maintain some distance—it just felt more companionable to speak about touchy subjects without the entire room, small as it was, between them. "I know it's not my business..."

"But you're going to ask anyway. So, here's the summary. My father died this past winter. We hadn't spoken since I graduated high school and went to college. He told me not to come back if I left, and I didn't."

"You must have had a pretty big fight for it to come to that." He was bothered. Mr. Shoemaker was bothered. She was bothered. Time to stop asking about this stuff.

"Yes." He didn't elaborate.

She really shouldn't press. She didn't want to know, but she also didn't want to see something hurting him either. "I don't talk to my parents that much, but we're just distant people, I guess. Email every month or two. They travel around even more than I do. I never quite know where they are."

"Why do they move so much?" Wyatt asked, some of the stiffness subsiding when the subject shifted away from him.

"I never really figured it out," Imogen said, realizing after the words were out that she'd just admitted her reasons were different than theirs.

There was a strange look on his face she couldn't identify, and it made the silence feel heavy and in need of being filled.

"I didn't like moving around when I was a kid. It was hard. But I guess that's just who I am now."

He crossed his arms and leaned against the counter. Said nothing.

"Tried to settle down once. It didn't take." He had to say something. This was about Wyatt, his father and Mr. Shoemaker, not her. "Your mom's gone, right?"

"Since I was young."

Aside from the weirdness of her spontaneous confessions, Imogen didn't know how to feel. Just bad, bad for the man and the boy he'd once been. "I'm sorry. Feel like I should know what to say to make you feel better, but I don't."

"You know how you can make me feel better, Emma-Jean." His voice dropped and he closed the distance between him.

Heaven help her, he was going to lay another knee-buckler on her when a patient might come in at any second. And, worse, she wanted him to. Even with his offer being tied to emotions. "Wyatt. There's... I..." She fumbled around a little and he stepped back. With him no longer looming over her, she found her voice again.

"I'm not going to say that the idea doesn't appeal—it does—but I don't want you to get confused. I would be happy to curl your toes and let you forget whatever it is that's twisting you up, but that's the kind of thing that leads to messy feelings when it ends." Feelings. Strings. Strings all over the place. She liked no-strings arrangements.

"How considerate you are." She couldn't mistake the derision in his tone. "Don't worry, Emma-Jean. Sex isn't just good for numbing you. Like a drug, you can build a tolerance for it quickly. No relationship with you could ever be built to last. I'm surprised you even came to help out Amanda, truth be told. I'm thinking it all came at a convenient time and you had other reasons to take to the road."

"Don't you think it's a little early in our relationship for you to make sweeping declarations about my motivations? You barely know me." But she knew a mask-slip when she saw it. Grief. And anger.

"I'm sure you're right. I'll be in the front, catching up on paperwork. Let me know if we get any patients." He glanced at his watch and added, "If we don't have any more patients in the next half-hour, we'll get on the road. I'd like to stop by Bent Reed since we have some time to spare. Never know when we'll be able to make that stop and there are a couple of patients I'd like to check on."

He retrieved his tablet from a locked cabinet and headed for his chair.

Why couldn't she leave things alone? Shouldn't have asked those questions. Should've just told him about his future purchases, suggested they sleep together and shut up about everything else.

CHAPTER FIVE

A GREEN HIGHWAY sign announced they'd entered the booming metropolis of Bent Reed—prompting Imogen to look for the town. Wyatt slowed the bus and looked down the access road from the winding two-lane highway to the small community, checking the way before committing the bus to crossing the bridge.

"I saw the sign, but I don't see the town," Imogen said as they rolled over the narrow old bridge, hoping to draw him out of the brooding mood he'd worked himself into.

"It's up here on higher ground. And it's more like a post office and a few houses than a town. This creek floods all the time. That's why it's called Bent Reed. The vegetation on the creek bank is frequently smashed to the ground."

"I kind of gave up trying to decipher the town names around here after we went through Pruedon-Fonde, Fleming-Neon and Pippa Passes... Not to mention all those different

Creeks and Hollows." She smiled. "But I like them. Begs a lot of questions."

"I don't know the stories of those towns," he muttered, pulling the bus into a gravel lot beside the post office and parking.

The next she knew, he was out the door, walking around, and leaving her to try and figure out what she should be doing. Set up on the chance they get patients? Wait to see if anyone walked toward them or pulled up and then set up?

With a sigh she went to at least get the usual equipment ready.

Wyatt stayed outside, prowling around, as if looking authoritative and impatient would make people flock to him to be healed.

Something moved in her peripheral vision, and she finally took her eyes from the tall, grouchy physician to see a mother with two children approaching the bus. The petite woman had an adolescent boy with her who rivaled her in height and a toddler on her hip, sporting a neon-green cast on one arm.

As the patients approached, Imogen hurriedly retrieved anything she thought Wyatt might need to see them.

She came out of Exam One as they stepped onto

the bus and the toddler immediately held out both arms, the broken and unbroken, toward Imogen as he leaned forward. More than leaning, he launched himself toward her. She dropped her stethoscope to catch him before he wriggled free of his terrified mom's grasp and broke something else.

"Someone's been watching too much Superman." Imogen chuckled, getting a better hold of the kid and settling him on her hip after his mother released his legs.

"He still doesn't have any fear of falling. Runs full tilt at stairs, the edge of the porch, anything. I swear he's gonna give me a heart attack." The woman pressed a hand to her chest and then bent to retrieve Imogen's stethoscope. "Hope that didn't break."

"They're sturdy. Let's go and see if he'll let us use it." Imogen grinned at the woman, who followed her into the exam room, along with the older boy.

"I'm Emily. This is Brandon. And you've got Michael." Emily made the introductions.

Imogen smiled at them, and by the time Wyatt had the charts, she had settled the tot on the exam table and ascertained the purpose of the visit.

"The cast is mighty itchy, Dr. Beechum," Imogen announced to Wyatt, and left Emily holding Michael on the table to step toward Brandon. The small exam rooms were tight with three people, so four and a toddler made it impossible to turn round. She laid a hand on the boy's shoulder. "Brandon, you want to come with me and have some juice while Dr. Beechum sees to Michael?"

"No. I want to stay," the boy said, shrugging out from under Imogen's hand, his eyes fixed on Wyatt and what he was doing. More male surliness. Imogen would put him at twelve, maybe thirteen. The age men learned to brood.

Emily gave Brandon a look but he didn't budge. To make more room, Imogen relocated to the doorway and waited to see if Wyatt needed her. She waved at Michael when he peeked around Wyatt at her, all two-year-old flirting eyes and smiles. Too cute.

Wyatt looked at something on the inside of the toddler's forearm and then at Brandon. "His arm's doing good. The itch is normal. He'll be okay," he said to the boy, who immediately brushed past Imogen and exited the room.

Michael picked that moment to wail, his eyes on the door his brother left through.

Imogen stepped back to watch him leave the bus

completely and then stepped back into the room. "He went outside," she explained after Wyatt and Emily both gave her curious looks. To quieten the screaming toddler, she took her stethoscope back to him and handed it over. Bright pink, made of rubber…kids loved stethoscopes. At least enough to stop crying.

They continued talking about ways to soothe the toddler's itchy arm, and the main condition—his idiopathic epilepsy—but today's visit was primarily about the itchy cast.

"If your hairdryer has one of those cold-air buttons, shooting it down the inside of the cast to help keep it dry will help. A children's painkiller might help as itching is a kind of mild pain." He gently put his big hand over Michael's head. "Distraction. Not as easy but effective."

Michael yelled for Imogen, not by name but with arms outstretched. She walked over to pick him up. Kids were the best. If she could handle the idea of moving one around, as she had been, she'd jump at the chance to be a mom. Stints in pediatrics here and there was the best she could do, and she frequently sought out those jobs when her life felt too messy and strained. The younger the child, the more honest their personality. In her line of work

the ones she found who hid their true feelings behind a mask usually did so nobly. Brave fronts.

Michael laid his head on her shoulder and she
rubbed his back and rocked as Wyatt discussed
the treatment with the tired mom.

"Come on, Amanda. I'm your best friend. You can
tell me who he is," Imogen said, sitting on the bed
with her friend and leaning back against the headboard. Amanda's mom was out doing the shopping,
and that left Imogen with some free time to hang
out with her bed-resting buddy—a solid block of
time when she could try and weasel out of her who
the daddy was. And, more importantly, what was
wrong with him.

"He doesn't need to be spoken about," Amanda
said, leaning against her propped-up pillows. There
was a strong resemblance between Amanda and
Wyatt, the same near-black hair and eyes, although
Amanda's lay straight like silk and Wyatt's was
prone to curling.

"You don't have to tell me what he did. Just who
he is." Imogen waved a hand, staving off the ob-
jection. "If you're not planning a wedding, I know
it's him. You're Happily-Ever-After Girl, with the
power to leap altars in a single bound."

"Not anymore." Amanda tried to wave the subject away. That wasn't going to fly with Imogen.

"If you're having a baby by him and you don't want him around, he did something bad. It's my job to make sure you're safe. I need to know who he is so I know who to slap with a restraining order when he makes his move." When. Not if.

"Your logic is a mess. He isn't a danger. I don't need protecting. We will be fine. He doesn't factor into this. Really, it's better this way. We'll be better off alone, me and Mom and...the baby. Who I need to figure out a name for at some point."

"Lizzie or Oedipus," Imogen muttered.

"Lizzie?" Amanda asked.

"Borden," Imogen clarified. "Just in case the kid has to commit patricide later in life."

"Oh, shush, you. You have been around Wyatt too long. You're as grouchy as he is."

That effectively redirected Imogen's attention. "He's like that with you too? I thought it was just me."

"Usually. Hard to get him out of it," Amanda murmured. "I've tried. What happened? Give me something new to think about. Tell. Me. Everything. Without mentioning his genitals or anything graphic."

Imogen went with the subject change. She wanted to know about the surprisingly tight-lipped man as it was the only way she was going to figure out his mask system well enough to protect herself and still have a chance at some fun. Asking him anything directly would just set him off on a brood. "Don't worry. I haven't seen his genitals."

Yet. But she planned to. Even if she had to set a trap involving ropes, nets and a blanket of leafy camouflage, she would get that man into bed. So long as he wasn't quietly psychotic. Or clingy. She might not be willing to specialize in pleasing one man for the rest of her life, but keeping the pleasure completely physical meant she had skills. Pleasure could sustain her, and having skills meant she could always keep busy enough that she didn't have time to think about the kind of feelings that messed everything up.

One day of peace. That's what Imogen decided to give Wyatt. That decision was made in the morning. Leave him to growl around the mountain, chop wood, pretend not to notice that antique, powder-blue homage to mass transit, and do whatever it was a man did alone on a mountain when he was In. A. Mood.

The plan lasted until a little after lunchtime. The knowledge that Dr. Raw-and-Bleeding might be raw and bleeding to death, alone on a mountain-top after chainsawing himself, changed the plan. At least, that's what Imogen told herself as she drove up the steep gravel incline. If he hurt himself again, she wasn't going to stitch him up. It would be hospital time. Chainsaw wounds wouldn't be clean little slices.

As the sound of the engine died away, she grabbed the basket of sandwiches she'd brought along. Amanda said no one "came calling" un-invited without food. Apparently, that was where things had gone wrong on their first meeting. As Imogen had approximately three dishes she could make and none of them transported well, peanut butter and jelly sandwiches would have to do.

As she rounded the old bus, one thing stood out to her: the lack of a Wyatt. The front flap on his tent was unzipped and looked empty. The logs he'd been notching—and that she'd dragged the longest few yards ever—were all arranged at each side of the cabin, but there was no Wyatt in sight.

She climbed the short distance to the cabin and stopped, her head tipped to one side, hearing the distant growl of a chainsaw echoing in every direction. He was somewhere out of sight, with that damned chainsaw. Even further away from rescue should the fool hurt himself.

With a sigh, she grabbed a couple of bottles of water from his cooler, stuffed them into her basket and started to climb. Up to the top of the mountain, and then from there maybe she could figure out which direction the noise was coming from.

Nearly an hour passed before she managed to determine where he was and reach him, between the periods when he ran the chainsaw, making noise that allowed her to follow him halfway around the blasted mountain, and the periods of silence when she got terrible images of him lying bloody on the leaves, minus some part of himself. And she liked all his parts. At least, all the ones she'd seen. But the ones she hadn't seen directly looked pretty good too, from what she could tell while ogling him day in and day out.

"Wyatt!" She bellowed his name just as he was about to start the chainsaw up again amid the timber carnage he'd already wrought today. He either heard her or felt her staring at him across the swath of felled trees, because he took his earplugs out and turned around to see her.

"I don't need you, Imogen."

"No, you just need a babysitter. You're alone in the forest, this far from a rescue, playing with a chainsaw, and you don't see a problem with that? Seriously?"

"Men have been doing this kind of thing for aeons. You'd think women would have got used to it by now and stop worrying."

"Sure." It was so hard not to roll her eyes, and there was nothing she could do to stop her head shaking at him as she marched toward him. "I brought lunch." She climbed onto the back of a trailer hitched to a small four-wheeler and put the basket down. "I'm sure you're hungry. Everyone loves PB and J, right?"

"I'm in one piece. If I eat the sandwich, will you leave me here in peace?"

"Probably not." Imogen leaned back and wriggled around until she was comfortable. "Don't worry, I'm as dismayed to find me here as I am to find you here by yourself. We should both count ourselves lucky that I managed to wait until the day was half over before coming to see whether you'd chainsawed yourself to death or not."

Wyatt didn't say anything, just took a sandwich and a bottle of water and sat down to eat in silence.

"Are you annoyed with me?" Imogen asked, getting a peanut-butter sandwich of her own and taking a bite. Sticky peanut butter might not be the best food to eat when you might be shouting at someone any second.

"No."

"You seem so." She talked between bites. Very small bites and lots of water.

"You're just so damned pushy it makes it hard to be around you at times."

"I think I have been fairly unpushy with you. I mean, aside from making you let me work, which, by the way, is the weirdest thing anyone ever had to do—beg someone to let them do hard labor for free."

"I guess." He didn't want to talk. He didn't want her there. But he didn't have to get what he wanted all the time.

She ate the first half of her sandwich and let herself study him. "Amanda said the white block thing was a graveyard."

"Why were you two talking about that?" Danger. His voice was too quiet. Too level.

"Because you hardly give any information when I ask you questions." Imogen garbled her way through peanut-butter throat, reconsidering the other half of her sticky sandwich.

"And you never wonder why that is?" He shook his head, half snorting at her.

"I don't need to wonder, I know why. You don't want to talk about anything. I get it. Really. I don't want to know, but somehow I can't stop asking. I blame whatever instincts made me become a nurse."

"You're back to wanting to heal me." He looked over the trees he'd harvested, but not at her. He studiously avoided looking at her.

"No. Not really. Comfort, maybe. Understand, for sure. But I'm pretty sure no one can heal you but you." Imogen rewrapped the other half of the sandwich and set it back on the basket.

"So wise."

"You make it hard to like you."

"But you keep trying." He did look at her then with eyes blacker than the soil she'd spent an hour sliding around in to make it to his side, and she couldn't read them. Nothing past one simple imperative: Stay Away.

"I keep getting these snippets of information." And peeks at different Wyatts. She needed help sorting them out. "And everyone keeps telling me to take care of you. Plus, you have a mystery graveyard in the woods, which, by the way, is not at all serial-killer-like of you."

The bit about people telling her to take care of him sharpened his gaze, but he shifted past it to say, "It's old. If the person who started it was a serial killer, they lived and died in the seventeen hundreds, and are probably buried up there."

Apparently the graveyard was easier to talk about than him needing to be taken care of.

"Is that where your folks and brother are?"

Not that much better. He stopped talking, finished his sandwich in a big gulp with the help of lots of water and got off the trailer.

He wasn't going to answer. Today she'd found the stoic mountain man who didn't want her on his mountain again. And the only way to get anything from that Wyatt was to badger it out of him. One good thing about being prepared to leave in a couple months: she didn't have to worry so much about damaging a future relationship. And badgering him might actually do him some good. Brooding and being Dr. Stoic Face sure wasn't.

"I don't understand why that's a hard question." Aside from dealing with death, which maybe she could understand him avoiding. But months and years had passed... It seemed simple enough.

"It's not hard. They're not there. The last one buried on the hill was my dad's dad. And before him at least fifty years since the next last. My parents and Josh are buried in the township cemetery, like everyone else in the county has been for the last century." It was the most words she'd gotten from him since yesterday at noon. "Why didn't you ask Amanda these things? You two have obviously been gossiping."

"She doesn't say much, just told me about what the white blocks were up on the mountain. Pretty much everything else I asked her she said to ask you, and that it wasn't her place to say." Wyatt was the second thing Amanda had ever been tight-lipped with her about. Wyatt, and the baby's daddy. And both topics were so mysterious, and so obviously riddled with emotion, it made her want to know more—making her behavior as weird as Amanda's.

"And Josh?" A glance flicked in her direction for a bare second. So tense.

No one had told her his brother's name before, and Imogen realized she probably only had it now because Wyatt was angry and a little looser with his tongue.

"Mr. Shoemaker yesterday."

"I see."

Mr. Shoemaker, the man who had started this crank-fest while they'd played horseshoes. No doubt he did see. Now, if he'd just let her get a glimpse of the situation…

"He's concerned about you. And you know what? I'm concerned about you too." Though she didn't want to be concerned about this man. It was a slippery slope to get this involved in someone's old wounds. One week and she had managed to wrap herself up in the lives of two people. Who knew how long it would take to unravel this mess without someone getting hurt?

"Some people like to worry." Wyatt marched around the four-wheeler to the front, grabbed chain wound around a winch affixed there and pulled it free as he headed for the first felled tree. Imogen watched him wrap the chain around one end, then he returned to the recreational vehicle being misused for heavy labor, started it up and began the winch.

She picked up her basket and stepped back out of the way to let him work. If nothing else, she would be there when he got hurt. A week had passed since she'd stitched up his last injury—those stitches should be ready to come out soon.

She'd remind him later. After he stopped being so angry.

By the time he had the tree dragged to the four-wheeler and was uncoiling the chain to repeat the log-gathering procedure with another tree, the long blast of a car horn echoed through the hills.

Wyatt dropped the chain and stood up straighter, looking back in the direction of the cabin, instantly alert.

"What's that?" Imogen leaned away from the surviving tree and looked in the direction he did, as if an answer would come running that way.

"Car horn." He spoke slowly, thoughtfully, "That's how my family always calls their kids off the mountain. No one can hear yelling."

"Someone's at your house, blowing the horn for you?"

"Yeah. Sounds like it."

"Like an emergency? Who would…?" The words died in her throat. "Amanda."

Dropping the basket, Imogen broke into a dead run for the trees. She shouldn't have come. Amanda was her responsibility. And if Jolene had had to leave her during an emergency to come and get help… Terror clawed at her throat.

"Imogen. Not so fast. Be careful," Wyatt yelled

from behind her, leaving the machine and his tools behind to run after her.

"It's got to be Jolene." Amanda's mom would know how to call people off the mountain. Imogen grabbed trees to control her skidding during the steeper parts of the incline. There had been rain that week, not a massive amount but enough to soak through the usual deciduous debris to the loamy earth beneath. It made traversing the hills so much harder. Her favorite hiking boots helped, but sometimes all she could do was try to control her fall.

"Imogen. Careful. You're going to get hurt and that won't help Amanda." He sounded further away.

By the time she'd crossed a gulley down the mountain and got within sight of the old homestead, the stitch in her side made it hard to breathe. The third car in the vicinity, a beat-up SUV with camouflage paint, didn't belong to anyone she knew. The owner lay on his back several yards from the car.

"Wyatt…" she yelled, but didn't turn round. "A man down in your driveway." Right, great update. The man waved one arm in the air and she noticed the drastic size difference between it and the one flopped out on the ground beside him. She tried again. "Bad edema!"

Wyatt crested a final rise behind her and soon overtook her on the descent, "That's Ed Fuller."

Should she know Ed Fuller?

It felt like they'd been running for hours by the time she fell at Ed's side with Wyatt. One of the man's arms was immensely swollen and had marks on the hand and wrist.

"Doc?" Ed's voice rasped on the word.

"Ed, these snake bites?" It barely sounded like a question, like Wyatt expected Ed to sport snake-bites.

"One of my boys got me." The man drew ragged breath.

Wyatt loosed a slow controlled breath of his own out of flared nostrils—an angry bull.

"Airway." Imogen said the one word to Wyatt then bolted for her Jeep to grab her first-aid kit. Digging into it as she ran back, she grabbed a packet of antihistamine tablets and showed it to Wyatt.

He looked at the bus for a second and then back to the patient as Imogen placed the packet in his hand. A second later he got them in Ed's mouth. "Chew." And then to Imogen, "Water."

She dropped the first-aid kit and ran to and from the cooler, opening the water bottle to tilt it to Ed's mouth as she returned.

Wyatt grabbed a roll of gauze from the kit and wrapped a snug band above the wounds, not that it would do much good with the tissue swelling like that.

"You can sell the venom to make…shots for folks that get bit." Ed kept talking. She could hear the progressive squeeze in his voice as his throat constricted.

"What kind of snake, Ed? Rattler?"

"Copperhead. Don't milk 'em, but I like having them. Sets." He swallowed the water, or what he could of it, and started to wheeze, "I gotta tell you, I'm feeling kindly poorly this time."

This time?

"How many times have you been bitten?" That did sound like it surprised Wyatt, like it surprised her.

"By copperhead? Three? Four?" Swelling came over Ed's face fast and in a few seconds his lips were inside out.

"Oh, hell." Wyatt gritted his teeth, pointing at Imogen. "Watch him!"

Watch him what? Why had Wyatt gone pale?

Imogen reached for Ed's unswollen hand and talked to him gently while the suddenly wan Wyatt slammed the sliding door open on the ancient blue bus and banged into it. The whole beast tilted as he stepped inside—and that was all the Wyatt-watching Imogen had time to do. Ed worried her.

Still holding his good wrist, she kept count of his pulse, monitoring the speed and how fast it increased while she listened to his breathing. There was no time to engage her curiosity about the bus.

It sounded like Wyatt was tearing the place apart. She could hear slamming sounds as well as a steady stream of cussing.

"How are you doing, Ed?" His heart rate she estimated in the one-thirties and climbing. "Don't worry. We're going to get you patched up."

Just as she opened her mouth to shout for Wyatt, the back emergency door banged open and he jumped out with an epi-pen in hand.

"Where did you…?" She blinked at the injection.

"Dad had a bee allergy." He tore the thing open and jammed it into Ed's thigh. "This is adrenaline, Ed. It's going to help you breathe better. In a few seconds you're going to start feeling pretty jittery, but the swelling is going to go down fast. Concentrate on breathing, slow and deep. Your throat isn't closed, it just feels like that because the natural reaction to this situation is panic. It's open, just enough for you to breathe. Control the panic. You're a strong man, you can do that." He may have been lying a little, but it only took a few seconds for the adrenaline to kick in, and the diphenhydramine would help too.

He nodded to Imogen to take over the calming words while he turned to the first-aid kit. Out of the corner of her eye she could see him cleaning the tip of a very large pocket knife with an alcohol prep, getting ready to make Ed an airway if it came to it.

"Once you have a little easier time breathing." Talking gently she could do. Imogen took over, leaning in to block what Wyatt was up to. Comforting Ed was easy. Figuring out why Wyatt had gone pale before he'd gone into the bus was harder, and something she'd have to mull over later. After Ed didn't die. "We'll get you to the hospital so they can take care of the bite for you. I imagine it burns."

When Ed started to breathe a touch better, Wyatt looked at Imogen and nodded to the Jeep. "You have room for two in the back?"

"It's got stuff in it." A pause and she clarified, hoping not to sound panicky, "Some boxes. Truck?" She should've already taken the stupid glass collectables out of the car. It had just felt weird to move them into Amanda's house. Permanent. Like she was staying.

Wyatt looked at Ed's vehicle, which also looked loaded down in the back with something, "What's in your car, Ed?"

"Aquarium with the snake," he whispered, then added, "Don't tell my wife. Suzanne'll kill me…"

"Truck?" Imogen blurted out her suggestion again. They could squeeze in…

"Only holds two in the front, Imm." Wyatt finished wrapping Ed's arm and hooked an arm around the man's waist to help him rise, but kept his eyes on Imogen. "We're breaking the law, honey. Climb in the back and help me slide him in."

Imogen lowered the tailgate and climbed up into the back of the truck. When Wyatt lifted Ed onto the tailgate, she hooked her arms under his and slid him back so the gate could be snapped back into position.

"Is this a good idea?" She sought Wyatt's gaze as he headed for the driver's door.

"Do you trust me, Imogen?" Wyatt held her eyes, and though his were still that same impenetrable black, there was clarity and purpose in the shadowed depths. It comforted her.

Besides that, anything but "Yes" would worry Ed. "Yes." And the truth was she did trust him. It was ridiculous to trust someone not to crash and kill you when you never knew how other people were going to drive or the random things that could happen, but the look he gave her was so steady and confident she'd probably have ridden in the back of that truck all the way to Lexington without much persuasion. All he'd have to do was say things would be all right.

This mask was a nice one, but she couldn't identify it and didn't have time to try. Focus on Ed. Put all this business in the old-bus file and stop thinking about it. No time.

"Plant your rear behind the wheel well and keep an eye on him. I'll get us to the fire house and they can call the chopper. This is not a usual reaction to a copperhead bite." Wyatt added, "Anaphylaxis. Bang on the glass if you need me."

If they got past the window of effectiveness on the injection and Ed's airway started to swell shut again, she'd need him. Imogen nodded and did as she was told, smiling at Ed as she braced one leg across his lap and kept him anchored to her.

"Don't worry. You've got a doctor and a nurse looking out for you. I'll keep an eye on you back here, we'll have a little adventure in the back of a truck, and not worry because Wyatt knows what he's doing. Good driver. He drives that bus everywhere, even down roads that don't look wide enough for it to go down. Though I have to say when you're feeling better I think you should consider a change of occupation, Ed."

"Hobby." Ed whiffled a tinny laugh. He couldn't be more pale, his breathing more labored—but there was air coming and going for now. "At least if the snake kills me, Suzanne can't skin me alive."

She kept one of his arms in her lap, her fingers pressed to the pulse point to monitor what she could of his vitals. "Just concentrate on breathing and tell me straight away if you start to have any trouble at all."

And she would mentally prepare herself for the likelihood they would be stopping to perform an emergency tracheotomy if the fire house was too far away.

In the excitement, Imogen had left her purse and keys in the front of her car. Wyatt opened the door and grabbed both to toss them into the safety of the cab of his truck, which he could lock securely. He might feel safe enough there to sleep in a tent a few days a week while working on the cabin, but he wouldn't be responsible for her belongings—especially since he'd sent her on to the hospital with Ed and had come home. Neither of them had taken time to close doors or gather personal belongings before they'd torn out of there for the fire station.

Logs. The cabin. The four-wheeler. All these things he could control. He needed to control something. Since he'd entered his dad's bus, everything had felt distinctly out of his control.

Grabbing a bottle of water, he began the long climb to where he'd abandoned his tools to chase car horns and Imogen down the mountain.

He couldn't control the woman; she could barely control herself. It was no wonder she moved so frequently. Probably just another form of her poor impulse control—she'd get the urge to go and see the world's biggest ball of string and off she'd go.

The familiar burn of the muscles in his legs, the roughness of the bark of trees he passed, the smell of the earth and the moss growing on the north side of everything…the mountain—his mountain—could almost fill a man. It always brought a measure of peace. He used it to put her out of his mind—just like he was trying to put the bus out of his mind.

It had been the right call, grabbing Dad's epi-pen. Resenting Ed for having made him go into the bus to retrieve it wasn't rational. Even now, hours later, in the forest, if he didn't focus on the scents surrounding him, it was the memory of stale ciga-rettes and whiskey that filled his nose. The musty smell of old furniture and tang of coal left in the bucket beside the pot-bellied stove from last win-ter—a reminder of the last time anyone had en-tered that damned bus.

He tried not to think about the pictures on top of the old console television that had broken in his youth and which now served as the stand for a small working television. A few photos of him, a few of Josh, snapshots and Polaroids, yellowed as much from the environment as time.

Reaching his site, he took inventory to be sure all his stuff was still there, picked up Imogen's basket and put it on the seat of the four-wheeler, along with the chainsaw, and began hitching logs. Getting the logs hitched to haul to the chute he'd cleared early in the building process.

With his body engaged in labor, his mind wanted to wander, and it always went to those dark corners of his mind. So much regret. If his thoughts didn't go to Dad, or to the emptiness of the mountain after centuries of family that had lived and died there, he thought of Imogen. She was better to think about. A woman like that could make you forget. He hadn't been very nice to her and, as annoying as she could be, she also had been very helpful. Kind, even. He'd make it up to her for this Ed business. Later. Tonight. Tomorrow... Some time soon.

CHAPTER SIX

GLASS RATTLED IN the backseat of the car, sounding entirely too breakable as Wyatt maneuvered Imogen's girlish nightmare of a vehicle off his mountain. It continued rattling for the duration of the trip to Amanda's house, where Imogen was staying.

The purse, bane of every man's existence, needed to be carried in. With a grimace, Wyatt tucked it under his arm and lifted the boxes of breakables to take them in too. Helping her unload was the least he could do.

Tonight he didn't even let himself in. He went to the front door and knocked. When she opened the door, he almost choked. Denim shorts. Red, white and blue bikini top.

"I brought your car," Wyatt said by way of a greeting, unable to come up with a single other thing to say.

Her look skewered him. She dropped one hand to her hip, drawing his gaze to that lovely curve from waist to hip. When the door rattled, he noticed she was holding it shut and looked back to her eyes through the mesh barrier.

"Did you bring me flowers and an apology for abandoning me with your patient?"

"I can do one of those. Didn't bring flowers." He looked pointedly at the handle of the screen door and back to her. "Can I come in?"

"Strange question: Why don't you stink?" Imogen didn't open the door.

"I took a bath?" Did he usually stink? She did come to the mountain a lot when he was working...

"Where? Did you sneak in and bathe while I was away with your patient?" Okay, she was definitely angry. And maybe a little irrational.

"I did not sneak in and bathe while you were away," he said, and smiled, trying to encourage one from her. "I washed like a pioneer."

"And that means?"

"In the creek." Getting her into her usual sassy, playful mood might not be easy tonight. "I can't sleep in that tent when I smell like I've been working all day."

His attempt to joke around won him enough ground that she opened the door. Well, she pushed it open wide enough for him to get his foot inside and keep it from slamming. Before he could get another word out she turned away from him and went to the kitchen.

Her hair was piled on top of her head in a wobbly tangle that drew his gaze from the baby-fine hairs at the nape of her neck, all the way down that beautiful, supple back that had nearly broken him. Why was he here again?

"I didn't expect to see you. I thought you'd stay holed up in the woods, brooding and hating everything until I came to roust you out again or until you had to work." She pointed to the table. "Be careful with the boxes, please."

Oh, right. Quell her anger. Maybe apologize. "It's pretty late," Wyatt said, fighting his thoughts back with effort. "If you were going to roust me out, I figure it'd have been earlier."

"Good guess. I'm doing dinner tonight to take to Amanda and Jolene. It really isn't the best time for me to leave the stove and make a twenty-minute round trip to take you back up the mountain."

"I can wait." He cleared his throat. "Or I can come back later, or visit Amanda and Aunt Jo if you want me out of here."

When she didn't answer, he nodded toward the

boxes. "Why did you pack glasses and then not bring them in?"

"They're teacups. Some spoons. The newer pieces are mostly thimbles and a few things that fit into the novelty category more than anything else."

Whatever she was making smelled good. He tried to focus on that rather than all that soft skin. "Why do you carry them around?"

"They're mementos from the places I've lived so I don't forget where I've been." She put the lid back on some kind of tomato concoction and went to the table to open the box. One by one, she pulled out different things—some of which were still wrapped in newspaper and some of which had rattled free of their protective wrapping. On the bottom of one box lay a large glass case. She took it out, set it on the table and then began unwrapping pieces to place inside.

City after city—shiny breakable advertisements for the nation's most popular tourist sites all went into the case in a particular order. A timeline set in ceramic, criss-crossing the country.

He didn't say anything as she worked, moving them, shifting the lot to the side whenever she found she'd skipped one—all this organization took time and a good memory. All except a tiny piece of stoneware crockery that claimed to hold Wisconsin cheddar. That one, she kept in her hands and fiddled with it, but she didn't flip the little metal latch to remove the lid.

"How many places have you lived?" He started to count when they were all in place.

"Oh, I have no idea. I went to two or three schools every year until college, and then I was there for two years with Amanda, and then back on the road again."

Her words took the air out of him as effectively as the punch he'd spent the week expecting and it took him a minute to figure out why.

Always the new kid. He'd never changed schools before college, but he'd been through the routine in enough hospitals with Josh. Sometimes Josh was the new kid, sometimes he just wanted to meet the new kid, and every meeting was strained by sickness. He couldn't imagine a worse way to spend your whole life. Loneliness was a sickness too. He saw the symptoms every day, here and there. She managed them, but they were still present.

No wonder she had dropped everything and come running when Amanda had needed her. His throat closed enough that he had to cough to clear it. "If you didn't like it then, why do you keep it up now?" He spoke slowly, carefully, hiding how her careless words had affected him.

"I like it now. But maybe someday I'll find somewhere to settle. When I find the perfect place. Don't just want to settle on a place to settle. You know? You can settle down somewhere without settling for somewhere you won't really be your happiest." She fiddled with the little piece of crockery, repeatedly flipping the latch open and closed.

Her tone was off. Wyatt had spent enough time with her since she'd arrived to know the ring of falsity in her voice. Emptiness. Like hearing a parrot speak, the sounds made words but lacked conviction. Why would she lie about this? "What does a place need to be perfect? Is it country or city? The climate? Culture?" He played along.

"No." Imogen shrugged, but didn't look at him, her attention supposedly on her tasks. "I like cities okay, but I usually bounce between city and more rural venues. Like the last place I lived before coming here was Chicago, and before that I lived in a little nowhere place in Ohio nestled amid a bunch of state parks and cave systems. Before that, Atlanta."

"Where in Atlanta?"

"North side." She turned back to the stove and checked the dinner again and put the cheese container on the counter beside the stone, making it hard for him to inspect the thing.

He had been in Atlanta during that time. Weird to think they could have seen one another. He'd have remembered if they had. Whether her hair had been blonde or pink as it had been, Imogen stood out for more than hair color and height. Silence stretched, and he realized he should've said something when she'd glanced over her shoulder and caught him staring at her.

"Why do you really move around so much?" Wyatt asked when she met his gaze.

"I told you." Imogen looked away. She didn't like to look at him when she lied.

"You told me something," Wyatt murmured. She didn't like to talk about herself. At all.

"Do you want to stay for dinner?"

The subject change was expected but not unappreciated.

She tilted her head to shoot him a sidelong grin. "We need to talk."

The look said she was referring to the time when he'd said the same and had then promptly accosted her with his mouth.

If he was honest with himself, that offer wasn't unappreciated either. "Talk like you talk, or talk like I talk?" Wyatt grinned at her flirty over-the-shoulder looks. She might be distracting him on purpose. Hell, knowing her penchant for tricks, she was definitely distracting him on purpose. But it was a good tactic. Even without makeup and smelling like coconut, she was damned distracting.

"Like you talk." She went about dishing food into portable containers, and after they were loaded on a tray surreptitiously stuffed the small container into her pocket. That wasn't suspicious at all…

"After you apologize for dumping me with poor Ed earlier. He's okay, by the way." With her tray loaded and her cheese crock with her, she stepped through the back screen door—the quickest route to Jolene's, next door. Through the screen, she smiled at him. "And just so you know, if you stay, you're definitely getting lucky."

She disappeared before he could think of a suitable response—or a suitable reaction. Just left him trying to remember why his reaction shouldn't be *I'm sorry. Take off your top.*

"You're still here," Imogen said as she stepped back inside the small cottage to find Wyatt precisely where she'd left him: standing in the middle of the kitchen, dominating the space. Had he changed his mind about wanting her, or were the immobility and weird expression for some other reason?

"I drove your car over," he reminded her, "so I either have to stay until you drive me back or I have to walk back to the mountain."

She closed the door and approached him. Although dusk had turned to darkness, August in the South was hot enough that the night air was still heavy, wet, and warm. As she walked closer, she barely resisted the urge to put a little extra wiggle in her walk. The man was already fighting to keep from looking at her chest, something that pleased her and went a long way toward assuring her he hadn't changed his mind about his desire.

"Are you hungry?" Food. Other stuff. Both good with Imogen.

"Yes." Back to one-word answers, but a new intensity stayed his tongue tonight—not a trace of anger or smugness, the masks she mistrusted.

She reached for his chest, running her palms up to his shoulders and around. He wanted her, and he'd made the first move, so it was her turn. "You know, you could kiss me again. If you wanted."

His lips pressed together but his hands fell to her hips, nicely contradicting himself.

"That was a hint." She jostled him slightly, smiling at the big, silent man. Big, silent, firm man. She ran her hands over his shoulders again, one finding the back of his neck to knead. The nerve it took to make the pass was worth it, just to see the way his breath quickened, to feel his chest rise and fall against hers. But he didn't make a move, just stood there staring at her as he had before the kiss on the bus—like he was dividing fractions in his head.

She leaned up and kissed the side of his neck, where the beard he kept so close faded to skin, triggering his large hands to slide to her hips and squeeze.

"Imogen."

His voice sounded so strangled she leaned back to look at him. "What's wrong?"

"I'm not sure this is a good idea." His hands kneaded even as he spoke, a little wrinkle forming between his brows.

"Your hands disagree." It was cute when he played hard to get. Inexplicable, but cute.

With a breath he nodded and slid his hands up her back and down her arms, and the large, hot hands curled around her elbows and urged her arms back down.

"What?" She stayed where she was, their bodies lightly skimming where flesh rounded out, but she removed her hands at his urging.

"If we're together, people will know it and start making wedding plans."

That got her attention…at least, until it started sounding like a trick. "If you don't want me, just be a man and say it."

"That's not it." Wyatt shook his head, looking at her oddly, like she was the one pulling a fast one. "It's not as simple as that." He licked his lips, pausing a long moment before he explained. "You muddle my thinking. When you don't get your way, you argue relentlessly, and that's without having relationship leverage."

"Relationship leverage? You're seriously overestimating my intentions." She waved a hand, backhanding the air. "Whatever. Say you're sorry about earlier, even if you don't mean it."

He scrubbed a hand over his face and lowered his voice to a calmer level. "Ed was out of danger with you and the medics. I knew you could handle it. I needed to get away."

"So, it was because of the bus." Imogen focused

on that topic. It was easier for her to think about. Shouldn't have been, but it was. Not quite so fresh, and it didn't amount to him not liking who she was or how she acted. And it wasn't even accurate. What had she done after that first day on the mountain to earn such judgment?

"I had work to do," Wyatt corrected.

"You didn't have to go back to the mountain to chop down trees that badly. Want to tell me what happened on the bus?"

"No."

Imogen shook her head, not really knowing what else to do about his stubborn streak. "Fine." Never mind how frustrating it was to try and get information from a man who seemed to delight in being as taciturn as possible.

"What, you're not going to torture it out of me?"

"Why bother? You do need to talk about it," Imogen announced, but was quick to add, "But I'm not going to make you. You're a very big boy and it's your business."

"Why is this any different than any other situation where you don't immediately get your way?"

"I don't know, but it's different." Imogen stepped away, pushing back the short, tickling hairs from her face.

"How?"

"Because I don't want to know. I do, and I don't. I don't because the more I know, the more I care, and I frankly don't want to care that much." Shouldn't have said that.

"Makes it harder to leave?"

And now he was looking smug? Oh, hell, no, he should still be looking contrite. "No. Makes me want to leave faster."

"Then what the hell was all this?" Wyatt demanded, his arms crossing over his chest, which only drew attention to his stupidly wide shoulders.

"That's just sex, Wyatt." A little impulse control would be good right about now. Too bad she'd used it up earlier. "I'm not going to spend the coming months celibate. And as I muddle your thinking with my tantrums and whatever, I'm sure I can find someone else to occupy my down time."

"I never said tantrums," Wyatt muttered.

"Okay, you implied. Since we're getting so technical. If someone always has to have her way, it sure seems in the neighborhood of Tantrum City." Not that his opinion mattered. He couldn't hurt her. She wasn't hurt. That would violate her first rule: don't get too close. Sex controlled relationships for her, physical affection rather than the other messy emotions. Except he'd denied her that. So maybe that was the problem.

"What do you call this? Not a tantrum because you didn't get your way?"

"Oh, my God, this is not because I didn't get my way. And for the record, I've been here, like…five minutes and I'm certain your patients don't see me in the disparaging way you do." He might hate her tomorrow, but he needed to hear this. And in a few months it wouldn't matter if he hated her or not. His practice would benefit from him loosening up. "In fact, they like me better than they like you."

"No. They don't. They're just humoring you. Because they're nice people."

"Something you could learn from them. But then you couldn't be superior and abrasive with everyone. For all the talk of you wanting your patients to think of you as family, you do everything you can to make sure they don't."

His jaw clenched, chewing on nothing again, the way he had with Mr. Shoemaker. The flared nostrils and coal-black eyes were new, just for her.

Maybe she was going too far. Her eye twitched, prompting her to rub it and scale the argument back. Making him too mad would ensure her point was missed. And the point was valid, no matter how they'd gotten round to it. "They want to like you, but you're pretty severe and tight-lipped with them. People don't like conflict. If it seems like you'll break into a lecture, they keep their heads down and their mouths shut."

With a grunt he unfolded his arms, probably trying to look less severe. But his unfolded arms didn't really help. They hung like those of a fighter ready to throw or block a punch. "I don't think that's true."

"So I'm either lying or stupid? Narrow-minded. And there's a difference between confidence and arrogance."

His expression shuttered. "Not stupid, just wrong. You don't know the area or the people well enough to diagnose my practice problems."

"But you agree there are problems." Imogen shook her head. "Of course, you're right, Dr. Beechum. That is the mask I'm talking to, right? Of all your different faces, I like this one the least."

"Take me home," he said, grabbing the keys off the table, "or I'm taking your ridiculous purple car and leaving. Make your choice, Emma-Jean."

"My name is *Imogen*." She prowled past him and into the kitchen. "I'll pack dinner up for you and get you to your stupid mountain. If you take my car, I'm calling the cops."

"Forget dinner. I've lost my appetite," he yelled, loud enough to make her ears buzz even a room away. "And it's the sheriff around here. Not the cops. You call the sheriff."

"I don't care, Doctor. I'll take whoever 911 sends," she yelled back, banging through the cabinets to box and bag the food he would take with him. "You'll take the food, otherwise you'll just eat a bunch of junk. More takeout. Or maybe I'm wrong. Maybe you'll kill a bear with your pocket knife like the pioneers did it!"

She thrust the bag of food into his hands as she stormed past. He'd eat it if she sent it with him, because she sure as hell wanted him gone. He needed to get away earlier? Well, he could just stay away. She'd stay away too.

Her timing may have been bad, telling him the truth in anger, but it was still the truth, no matter the volume or rationale for telling it.

She ducked into the bedroom to grab a shirt then snatched her keys from his hand and went outside, leaving him to follow. "Oh, and it's time your stitches came out. Something I can *legally* do for you tomorrow, before work. I should be past the

urge to stab you with something sharp by then."
Something *else* she was right about.

But he was probably right about them messing around. Lust had got the better of her. Messing around would encourage him to mess with her plans, like he'd undoubtedly messed with her car. She'd probably have to readjust everything after he'd driven it. And messed everything up.

They drove in silence, the only noise inside the car the sound of the engine and through the open windows the songs of nocturnal creatures in the countryside. It should've been peaceful, but it just felt bad.

Tomorrow she was going to be the distant and terse one. See how he liked it. One-word answers. Yes. No.

He climbed out of the car in his drive and she thrust the bag of food at him again. One hand closed around the bag while the other sat atop the doorjamb. Wordlessly, he stood for several seconds before managing, "Thank you."

She probably should say something to that, but her well of words had finally run dry.

The door still stood open with him, watching her. She looked at the dash, her hands white-knuckling the steering-wheel, not up to even a single-word answer. The food she'd given him smelled rotten, the scent she usually loved making her feel nauseous. She looked out the opposite window, swallowing and waiting for him to close the door.

"It'll be better like this. Keep things professional. Nothing will get confusing." Wyatt's voice was calm, so much calmer than anything she could muster. Doctor Face knows best.

A nod and she put the vehicle in reverse and gave him a few seconds to close the door.

See, she could be terse.

She could be almost mute when her feelings were hurt and words failed her.

With more family in the area than Imogen could likely imagine, Wyatt did the smart thing the following morning and went to his aunt's house to shower. Nothing had felt right since he'd gotten out of Imogen's car. It was like someone had moved the furniture in his house one foot to the left but he still operated by the old floor plan. It left him feeling awkward and bumping into everything.

This off feeling intensified when he left Jolene's house and noticed that Imogen's car was gone. Not a single light burned in Amanda's house. Not even the porch light shone in the early twilight hours when a porch light would be beneficial. A sick feeling came to his stomach. Had she left?

That might be the kind of thing she'd do, and after the weird argument they'd had he could believe she wouldn't say boo to him before going. But not Amanda. She'd talk to Amanda.

Or maybe she'd call Amanda from the road.

With more speed than was strictly acceptable, he climbed into his truck and got it on the road. Ten sick minutes later he pulled into the lot where he kept the bus and found her parked on the far side of it, waiting for him. Early. Nursing a tall cup of coffee.

"Morning." Not awkward at all. He unlocked the door and held it open for her.

She didn't even look at him as she went inside. "Do you want to get the stitches out before we get on the road?"

"Yeah, that would be a good idea." He unbuttoned his cuff and rolled up the sleeve, exposing a fresh bandage placed there after his morning shower.

She put her coffee down, washed her hands, then went to get the supplies necessary to get it handled, not speaking again until she was gloved and had scissors and grips in hand. "Do you want to watch in the mirror?"

"No. You know what you're doing."

A terse nod and she set about snipping each stitch and gently extracting it. No matter how angry with him he could see she still was, she treated him with the kind of soft, steady touch that made him wonder if she'd gotten started at all when she announced she was done and shuffled the old stitches off into the waste.

He unrolled his sleeve and she turned back, swab in hand and gauze, ready for a new dressing. "The stitches are bleeding a little. Might stain your shirt. Do you want it dressed?" No telling him anything today, as deferential as he'd wanted from the beginning.

"Didn't feel anything, didn't realize it was bleeding. Dress it," he answered, and a half beat after that added, "Please."

Cleaning and dressing took hardly any time, and then she stepped away to clean up before they got on the road. It was a rare thing for her to be in the vicinity and not talking. Wyatt felt an alien vacuum, the kind that made him want to spit up words randomly. The kind that made him thankful when he finally got behind the wheel of the bus and it roared to life.

Imogen slept again. She was good at that, and tended to doze off every time they were in motion for more than fifteen or twenty minutes. Her unconsciousness made the silence a little easier, but not much.

She'd relax when they got to work, and the tension would fade. Professional distance was better, and also what he wanted. This interim period? Growing pains. That's all it was.

CHAPTER SEVEN

HOW LONG COULD she give him the cold shoulder?

Three days and counting.

The stubborn woman had lied about torturing him. Two people could be professional and nice without flirting.

She could look at him every now and then, for crying out loud.

As the day wound down Wyatt stepped into Exam Two to find his three favorite senior sisters sitting, standing, and taking up most of the space in the room built for three or four max—making it five with Imogen and himself added to the mix.

As always, they were nicely dressed, and each had freshly laminated, helmet-like grandma hair and red lipstick. They might look enough alike to pass for triplets but there was at least nine months and a couple of days between each of them. They did everything together—including doctors' visits, as much as he'd tried to dissuade them the first couple months he'd seen them. They'd have abided by his request if he was as scary to the patients as Imogen claimed he was.

As she took vitals, Imogen laughed at a story the three of them told, half the time in unison. Some tale about the brazen hussy involved in a love triangle at their seniors group and the scandal that had erupted at their regular weekly trip to the local music hall. Silly for that to annoy him. Imogen did what he told her to do—made the patients like her. But did she have to laugh with them and enjoy it so much?

Not one of the four women had looked at him since he'd stepped in, but they genuinely liked Imogen. Granted, they were exactly what he expected Amanda to be like in fifty years—friendly to a fault. But you could be friendly without being affectionate. They loved her. And she liked them too, he could see it in her smile—but that had been before she'd looked at him and it had vanished.

"Misses Arminda, Estaleenie, and Genoie." Imogen even said the names right, despite the spelling being off in the same way the spelling of his last name differed from the way it was said in the area. A situation he'd thrust Imogen into when he'd started calling her Emma-Jean.

"Afternoon, ladies. Who wants to go first?"

He stepped in but leaned to one side so Imogen could get past him in her flight from the room. She brushed against him, unable to help it, and he caught a breeze of the fruity perfume she wore. Sweet, but with a bit of tartness to it. Fitting. And distracting.

She stopped at the doorway, making room but standing by in case she was needed.

No one volunteered, so he just took them in order, asking the usual questions and performing cursory checks. He made notes as he went, becoming more irritated with the fact they'd stopped chatting.

Imogen couldn't be right about them being scared of him. But maybe she was right about them not really liking him. Damn. Did she have to be right about stuff that annoyed him?

"So, which one of you ladies are the third part of the love triangle?" Maybe they just needed to know it was okay to talk to him.

"Genoie," two of them answered.

He wrote prescription refills—they liked to get them on paper still—and tried his best to keep the story flowing. "So, Miss Genoie, you and this fellow were dancing together..."

"Every week. Regular," Genoie answered.

"When this other woman…" They were slow to pick up his cues.

"She cut in." Arminda took the bait, finally. "And Genoie's not danced with him since then."

"Doesn't he ask anymore?" Imogen asked. She was throwing him a line, like he couldn't handle this on his own.

"Every time he looks at me, I look the other way," Genoie announced, all but harrumphing at the end.

"But if he asked you?" Wyatt asked.

"I'd say no. Unless he apologized."

Oh, hell, more apology business. He saw Imogen shoot him a smug look.

They saw it too and immediately three sets of pale blue eyes fixed on him, two through bifocals. "What'd he do, Emma-Jean?"

"He abandoned me and I had to beg for a ride back from far away," Imogen said.

They all gasped.

He could have choked her.

And he really didn't know whether to be glad she hadn't said he'd abandoned her with a patient, or in this manner that suggested he'd driven her out of state and made her hitchhike back. At least it didn't sully his practice this way. He supposed. "I thought she could handle it, and I had to leave."

The friendly-to-a-fault trio still looked mad at him.

"You'd better apologize for that," Genoie announced.

"You don't want to lose another nurse," Estaleenie threw in.

"I didn't lose Amanda," Wyatt argued. "She's on maternity leave."

"That don't matter," Estaleenie said, shaking her head at him.

"You'd better apologize," Arminda echoed.

Imogen looked at Wyatt, not saying a word, but he preferred it when her eyes called him an *ass* rather than this look of victory.

She may have won this round but the point was clear: they did like her better than him. And all this was her fault, making a mountain out of a molehill with the Ed business. Time to regroup.

Wyatt sighed, straightened from the counter and his prescription pad and turned to Imogen. "Miss Emma-Jean, I'm sorry I abandoned you and that you had to find your way home all by yourself in a new place. Will you forgive me?"

Imogen squinted slightly, but she nodded. "I

guess so, Dr. Beechum. I know you can't help it. It's just the way you are."

Right.

"Let me make it up to you. I'll take you dancing." He looked back at the sisters. "Where's your dance hall, ladies? Think it'd be okay with everyone if Emma-Jean and I came to dance tonight?"

"Tonight?" Imogen repeated. He could hear the hesitation in her voice.

"Oh, we'd love it for you two to come and dance with us. Now, this isn't that line dancing they do in Lexington. We two-step, and do proper dances."

"I love a good two-step." Wyatt winked at them and looked at Imogen.

"I don't think I have anything to wear." Imogen had probably never two-stepped.

"Any ole dress you got will look wonderful, Emma-Jean."

She was trying to think of a way out of it, he could see it in her wide eyes. They were all so happy to hear Wyatt was bringing her dancing, she couldn't say no.

"I have a couple of sundresses with me."

"That'd be just fine." The talk wound down after that, with Wyatt securing a ride from the motel from the sisters. Imogen couldn't back out then, and driving the bus to the dance hall would have seemed weird. There were no taxis in the area to speak of.

Arrangements made, they slipped out of the bus. As soon as they were gone, he felt Imogen's elbow sharp in his ribs. "That was dirty. I really don't have anything to wear to a dance hall, Wyatt. I don't think scrubs will do at all."

"You said you had a sundress."

"Do you know what a sundress is?"

"A dress." That you wore in the sun? "A dress is a dress, Imogen. Don't go kicking up a fuss about this. I'm doing what you told me to do."

"Which is?"

"Making friends with the patients."

She considered him, and by the look on her face she was considering where to hit him. "I don't know what you're up to, but if I'm going dancing with you, this is a work function. I'm on the clock, Dr. Beechum."

Pronouncement made, she went about locking the cabinets so they could leave.

"All right, I'll consider you a paid escort if you want. I think that might be against the local prostitution laws, but if you insist."

She threw a tongue depressor at him, bouncing

it off his cheek. He caught it and chuckled as he dropped it in the trash en route to the front. Locking things up took no time. All good design. A bus he could be proud of.

He started the engine, and soon she joined him in the front, seat belt on and arms crossed. His sign to get them on the road.

Imogen dug into her bag and pulled out one of the two cotton sundresses she'd brought. Scrubs were okay, but when she was in the motel after hours, she wanted to lounge about, and getting into her pajamas at six seemed way too early. Lazy.

But neither looked like the kind of thing she'd like to wear while mingling with patients. Unless it was a beach party, or something in the blazing-hot summer sunshine.

However, both could be useful for punishing Doctor Face Wyatt, if that happened to be the face she went dancing with. That was who had finagled her into this evening. Actually, that might have been a cross between Doctor Face and Charm Face, if the charm had been for her. It was too much to hope he was integrating his faces, he was just multitasking.

She shook out the black spaghetti-strap halter

dress, considering it. Was it more or less revealing than the one with the scrunchy top? Not so form-fitting. So…less?

Certainly not as loud as the other, which consisted of tiers of tiny floral prints.

Imogen went to work clean-faced, generally speaking. But if the cleavage was coming out, she'd make the most of her arsenal. By the time a knock sounded an hour later, she had her hair up in a summery tousle, smoky eyes and a deep red lip gloss that made her look like she was straight out of a blackberry patch.

A quick spritz of perfume, her feet crammed into sandals, and she stepped out.

"Did you go shopping?" Wyatt asked, frowning. He didn't have anything but his work wardrobe. Served him right. But his work clothes were usually slacks or black jeans and a button-down. She was the only one to wear scrubs.

"This is a sundress." She gestured to the top, obviously designed to maximize sun exposure.

"And you didn't want to wear that?"

"No. I had to borrow an iron from the front desk and this outing seems like it should be something you dress up for. Like church clothes."

Wyatt grinned and offered her an elbow. She didn't take it. This wasn't a date.

Work. Function. Only.

Wyatt overtook her and opened the car door for her.

Before she got in, Imogen hissed, "I'm serious. You wanted professional distance. You're my boss. This is me helping with your practice and image problems."

"Got it," Wyatt said. He was starting to believe that he had some ground to make up with some patients. And he knew for sure he had some to make up with Imogen.

No matter his proclamation about professional distance, he didn't at all like the way things had been going this week.

He slid in beside her, made his greetings and settled back to survive the somewhat nerve-racking forty-mile-per-hour drive to the dance hall. When they arrived, Wyatt got out, and kept the door open for Imogen, while making a quick lap around the car to open all the other doors.

The dance hall was a simple brick building with wooden floors, tables and a stage. As many people sat and watched the musicians as danced in the small dance area to one side. Wyatt swept Imogen onto the dance floor for a lesson in the two-step. She didn't even try to lead for once, and knew the dance already, which made it possible to settle in and talk.

"So what can I do about this scary image problem?"

"Stop scowling," Imogen said, a challenging lift to her chin.

He wove them through the sea of dancers, and then settled into a slower pace. Not plowing over a possible future patient while twirling a leggy blonde seemed smart, and might require more concentration than he was able to give with Imogen in his arms. "I'm concentrating, not scowling."

"Concentrate friendlier." She let go of his shoulder and with thumb and fingers nudged the corners of his mouth up.

"Brat." He smirked and leaned his head back.

"Jerk," she crooned back at him, making him smile for real. However he'd managed to get her there, she wasn't as angry as she'd pretended if that playful spark was there again.

"I've been promoted from *ass*." The song changed to something slower and he pulled her a little closer.

Imogen looked away from him, off over the people. "You know Amanda's baby-shower thing is next week with your family, while we're on the route?"

"I didn't know."

"Did you get her anything?" She looked back at him.

Wyatt found himself pulling her even closer, so the space between them disappeared, and he decided that he liked sundresses. Lots of skin to luxuriate in. His fingers brushed a cut-out in the back of her dress, unable to help himself. What was she talking about? Oh, baby gifts. "Uh, I figured I'd wait until it was born."

"Thought as much." She pressed a little closer, the hand on his shoulder creeping toward his collar. "One of the patients is making some baby things for you to give Amanda." Imogen's expression didn't match the confidence in her tone. There was something else there, but he couldn't quite put his finger on it. "She knits or something. Baby blanket. Little hat. Booties. Bibs."

"Oh. Thanks." Amanda would no doubt love the gift if Imogen had picked it out. He'd have probably got something unnecessary. As awkward as the conversation had grown, it was still much nicer than the week of ignoring him. The good it might do his practice was a clever cover. He really wanted to spend time with her.

"You're welcome." Her fingertips brushed the hair at the nape of his neck. She switched topics. "So you are going to be dancing with the other ladies tonight. During breaks, talk to the men. Oh, look, there's Mr. Shoemaker."

Wyatt looked in the direction she pointed. Standing a head taller than everyone else made it easy to see over people's heads. He and Imogen were probably the tallest people in the room. She had pulled back a little, enough to open a small gap between them. Gearing up to go and dance with someone else.

"You're all Glower Face again. Smile." Imogen jostled his shoulder, drawing his attention back to her.

Glower Face. Doctor Face. There was some truth to her claims that he wore masks. Right now he'd rather come up with some reason for her to keep dancing with him than the truth.

"Are you afraid he's going to want...?" She paused, the silence drawing his attention back. "Are you afraid he's going to want to talk about, you know...stuff?"

"No. That's not what I was thinking."

"Then what?" She kept dancing, and took the lead for a moment to turn them so his back was to Mr. Shoemaker.

"Never mind." He didn't need to make any confessions. At least not until he figured out how to handle her. At first he'd wanted to keep his distance so it didn't start any situations, especially with his family, who were trying to marry him off. Now knowing that Imogen was dead set on leaving in a few months, they couldn't be mad at him if she ran off like she always did and he failed once more to marry.

"No. Tell me." She pulled a lock of his hair.

Such a brat. An adorable brat. "No."

"Tell me or I'm going to cry and tell Estaleenie you said my dress makes me look like a fat hooker."

Caught by surprise, he laughed. She'd do it too, and the sisters were already mad at him over leaving her alone with Ed. "Maybe I'm thinking anyone else you dance with will get a close view of your chest."

"Jealous?"

"Terribly." He smiled again.

She laughed and pushed off his shoulders, stepping back. "Don't worry. I'm going to go sit and gossip, and look out for the brazen hussy who stole Miss Genoie's man."

A kiss on his cheek and she spun away in favor of the refreshment table.

Wyatt watched a moment then made his way to where the sisters sat and offered a hand to Genoie. "Honor me with a dance, ma'am?"

A minute later he was back on the dance floor, leading the tiny woman through a slow waltz. And watching Imogen.

She'd gone to speak with Mr. Shoemaker, and was now surrounded by a gaggle of men at the punch bowl, each vying for her attention. She was the only woman there under fifty, and there was the fashion-doll-like aspect. The tallness. The blonde hair. Those breasts...

"You don't like her talking to other fellers," Genoie said, drawing his attention back down. The top of her head came to his chest if he counted the hair. "You don't have to worry. Tall, good-looking boy like you. She's just putting you through your paces."

"Yes, ma'am. She is that," Wyatt agreed, leaning down a little so she could hear him. "She's been quarreling with me over the practice. Says I'm too grouchy. I scare people."

"Well…"

Dammit.

Genoie paused, and then drawled in a thoughtful way, "You do kind of make us nervous sometimes. We know you're a good doctor, though. Brilliant men can be hard to really know. The rest of us just talk and talk—don't have the sense to be serious, like a doctor. But I think you're doing pretty good. Today especially."

"Thank you, ma'am." Wyatt could hardly call a patient a liar, though she'd covered both sides of the argument diplomatically. At least she didn't outright take Imogen's side. She must be warming to him. And he really should take her opinion on board. "I'm trying to correct it. If you see me doing it again, you put me in my place."

"All right." She smiled at him. "I will."

He straightened, twirled her once and then leaned in again. "Which one is the brazen hussy?"

Over the next hour Wyatt circulated through the sisters, their other sisters, their cousins, their friends, their friends who were like cousins, and then he really needed a drink. He met Imogen at the punch bowl.

"It's Mr. Shoemaker," she hissed in his ear, her breath warm and sweet.

Wyatt leaned in, looking for the man. "With the brazen hussy?"

"Yep. And he's not a happy camper." Imogen looked like she was up to something. "I told him he should apologize to Miss Genoie, but his pride's all ruffled."

Wyatt could understand that. Right now he was thinking about how stupid he'd been to turn down the hot blonde in the bikini, and she would make damned sure his pride was ruffled when he admitted it.

"What should we do?"

"Not get involved," Wyatt replied.

"They want our help." Her eyes were bright. He may have tricked her into coming, but she couldn't be enjoying herself more.

He had to burst her bubble. Gently. "Not everyone wants your help, Imm."

"Maybe not, but they need it." She turned to face him and stepped in, hips first. Her belly brushed against his hips, but her shoulders pulled back so that the material of that dress pulled against her breasts.

The teasing light in her eyes told him she knew exactly what she was doing to him.

She leaned up, and he was drawn to lean in.

Every sparking inch of his being wanted to grab her hips and pull her harder against him, lose himself in the sweet scent of her soft flesh.

"Everyone would be happier if they just let me have my way." She let the tip of her nose tickle at the hollow beneath his ear, warm, moist breath fanning his flaming skin.

Kiss her. He could kiss her. Dance…it was practically expected.

"Ask Genoie to dance." The slow, mournful wail of a steel guitar announced the start of a slow song. "I'll ask Mr. Shoemaker and we'll meet in the middle." She spun out of his grasp before he could argue and swished away. Did her hips always sway like that when she walked?

Good grief, he'd turned loose a siren at the septuagenarian dance hall.

Wyatt groaned. But if he did what she said, at least he'd get to swap off and have her for another dance. He headed for the sisters.

The sisters stayed until nine-thirty, and then beckoned Wyatt and Imogen to follow them out to the car.

Once more, Wyatt sat in the back with Estaleenie, with Imogen between them, her long, lovely legs cramped where she sat on the hump. The angle of her legs caused the already short dress to slide up her thighs, exposing enough skin that his hand itched to touch the bare flesh.

Their fellow backseat passenger slept. No one would see if his hand wandered.

Reaching out, he rested his hand on her knee, fingers curling down to stroke the inside of her thigh. She sucked in a quick breath and turned to look at him, her lips parted.

"I feel like a sneaky teenager," Wyatt whispered, his nose touching the outer curve of her ear. "And I changed my mind."

"About?" Imogen whispered back. She knew the meaning of a hand on the thigh, but he would dance through some hoops after the way he'd behaved when she'd offered last time.

"I'd like *semi*-professional distance."

"What's that?"

"This thing where we feign professionalism by day, and by night you let me do dirty things to you." His hand slid up. Strong hands, and his fingers danced along the sensitive flesh, causing her heart rate to speed up and her body to come alive.

Imogen kept whispering as she reached to scratch lightly at the hair on his forearm exposed beneath the rolled-up sleeves. "I'll have to let you know if it's by night. We'll start on a trial basis. Two weeks to prove yourself."

He grinned at her and the memory of their first meeting. His smile and the strong hands squeezing sensitive flesh had the muscles in her belly quivering. "A month. Bare minimum for a decent trial." His fingers stretched, reaching the often overlooked underside of her thigh—which Imogen would've argued more intimate a touch than the inside.

One month wasn't three months, or six. That was still a fling. An extended fling maybe. But still a fling. As long as it was with this particular Wyatt she'd spent the evening with.

Her libido cooled briefly, the usual fears rising strongly enough for her to wrap her fingers around his wrist. "So long as I don't have to fire you spectacularly."

His questioning expression asked her to explain.

"I don't want to see Grouchy Mountain Face... or Doctor Face. Only Charm Face." The words carried too much weight. She thought for a second and leaned a little closer to his ear. "And Sex Face, obviously."

Wyatt laughed. Genoie turned to look back at

them. Wyatt drew his hand from Imogen's leg, like a good boy.

They drove the rest of the way in silence. Soon Arminda pulled off into the gravel motel lot and, after cheerful goodbyes, Wyatt escorted Imogen to the door.

The hand on the small of her back steered her for the rooms. Propelled her, really. Insistent. Electric.

The car didn't move.

"They're making sure we go to separate rooms," Wyatt said, snagging Imogen's key and unlocking the door for her. "They'll leave when we're both inside."

"You afraid?" Imogen asked.

He handed her key to her and stepped to his. "No, but you will be when they start making wedding plans."

"Good point," she stage-whispered. "See you in a minute."

He stepped inside after an intense, hungry look.

Inside her room, Imogen rushed to prepare herself. Sexy undies. Check. Robe. Check. Brushed teeth. Check. Hair down...

No reason to be nervous about this. Sex was sex. Being denied that release she needed was what gave his look the power to suck the breath from her.

Imogen opened the door and peeked out, making sure no one was around. A light in the bus made her hesitate. Was that Wyatt? Or was that someone breaking in to raid the drug cabinet?

Darn.

She wedged her sandal in the door and knocked on Wyatt's door. Nothing.

She looked back at the bus. Light off. Door opening. Big shadow exiting. Wyatt. What was he doing?

By the time she hobbled back to her door and got her foot back in her sandal, he was behind her, one arm around her waist, propelling her through the door.

She'd planned on going to his room. To have her exit strategy ahead of time.

The door closed and she opened her mouth to protest, but he had her in his arms and those sensual lips covered hers.

The man certainly didn't ease into kissing. It was all or nothing with him.

She could complain about the room in a minute. The taste of his mouth made her mind blank. The strong arms around her eased back and tugged the robe belt.

He lifted his head so he could see what was beneath.

"I put on something nice."

"Those pink shorts you had?"

"When you massaged me?" Imogen grinned as soon as the question was out. Hah, he'd been thinking about that too. "I can put them on if you like." The robe fell away to reveal the lacy panty set she'd donned and he shook his head, not disappointed in the slightest.

With skin bared, his hands greedily stroked her hips and around, tucking into the back of her panties to palm bare flesh. He pulled her hips to his, making her belly clench. She pawed clumsily at his shirt, getting buttons to give with brute force more than the kind of silken seduction she liked to practice.

What was wrong with her? She shook. Her heart pounded so hard she thought she might faint.

When her kisses turned more frantic, and her hands failed to reveal the chest she'd been thinking about since they met, Wyatt took over. His shirt came off. She worked on his belt. Something tore.

Material. Clothing. Not a big ripping sound, but it stood out. A seam.

When he'd tricked her into the dance, Imogen had been angry, but that had faded after lingering looks over the dance floor, the strength of his embrace as he'd led her through the dances. The way he'd made her move in concert with him.

Chemistry. Tension from the week before. The memory of his kiss. That's all it was. After they got past this first time, everything would relax. Everything would be okay tomorrow night. Easy. Playful. Not like this, twisted and needy.

Imogen tangled her hands in his hair, keeping his mouth with hers, every inch of her on fire, drunk on deep kisses and the soft scrape of the masculine dusting of hair on his body.

They'd waited too long. Anticipation gave power to his touch and the look of possession in his eyes. The need, though? Tomorrow night it would just be back to good, wholesome, toe-curling fun.

"Hurry." She bit the one word out, unable to stand any more, her feet sliding up the outside of his legs.

Within seconds he was inside her, his breath coming in short, hot blasts.

Every inch of her felt overly sensitive. Too intense. She closed her eyes, concentrating on the feel of his body against her, not the heat of his looks. This was a new face. If this was Sex Face, maybe she wanted Charm Face back.

Those black eyes absorbed her. She could feel his gaze as tangible as a touch even without seeing him.

"Look at me." His voice was thick, raspy and expected to be obeyed.

Imogen shook her head, even when he stilled. His voice turned silken. "Let me see those beautiful eyes, Emma-Jean."

She shook her head again, a little more frantic now that he'd effectively shut down her building orgasm. She wrapped her legs around his hips, urging him to move again as her hands found his cheeks and guided his mouth back to hers.

His tongue thrust into her mouth, drawing a painful spotlight on the rigid stillness he held over the rest of his body.

"Wyatt." Her voice was little more than a strangled plea.

"You'll be happier if you give me what I want." The stillness wasn't just hard on her. She could hear the tension in his voice, but there was no command in the words he used on her.

Her impulse control failed before his did. Imogen opened her eyes. The moment their gazes connected, he began to move again. Every frisson of pleasure was amplified by the look in his eyes, more intimate from the looking than anything she'd ever experienced.

God help her if it was like this every time.

CHAPTER EIGHT

IMOGEN AWOKE WITH a start. She'd fallen asleep? That had never happened before. Not since Scott.

The steady breathing at the back of her neck told her Wyatt was asleep too.

She'd had a plan. A good plan. But then there had been the kissing, and they'd been tormenting and teasing one another for hours, added to all those days of repressed sexual tension. And the vulnerability she'd felt with their eyes locked…

Worse, his big body was behind her, the heat of his skin and the soft scrape of his chest hair against her back. She didn't want to leave. She wanted to wake him up and see if the second time would be as devastating. In the name of science, of course. Not because she wanted it.

She could close her eyes and just go back to sleep. Ignore how safe and protected she felt with him beside her.

The fact that she wanted to stay meant she really

couldn't. She should get up and get dressed, take his key and sleep in his room.

"You're thinking too loudly," Wyatt mumbled, his lips at the nape of her neck. "Go back to sleep."

"I thought you were asleep," Imogen whispered. But now she had to stick with the plan. Changing the plan midway always caused problems.

"I was. I'm going back there."

"But this is my room." Imogen patted the arm draped over her waist. Her heart really wasn't in this escape. That scared her. "You have to go to your room now."

"It's the middle of the night," he muttered.

"It's one in the morning, and you're thirty paces from your bed."

"I like this bed."

"It's the same bed as yours." She stiffened and looked over her shoulder at him. Him arguing about it gave her the conviction to do what she had to do. The only safe thing to do. Just don't look him in the eye.

"This one is warm and there's a gorgeous blonde in it." He nuzzled again. "Is this how you usually do things? Love 'em and leave 'em?"

"Yes. Except for the love part." What had happened, what was happening, was freaky chemistry. And prolonged anticipation. The chase. She could make him let her up. "Let me up or tell me about the bus."

He grunted, buried his face in the pillow and called her bluff. "Fine."

Dammit! She shifted around until she faced him, shocked he hadn't put up a fight. A couple of inches separated them.

"The cabin got too unsafe to live in when I was a kid. Dad bought the bus and gutted it as temporary housing while he rebuilt the cabin." A pause and he added, "He never rebuilt it."

As he spoke, Imogen expected him to look at her, but he didn't. He lay there with his eyes closed, much as she had, and probably only answered as a way of bartering. His tone was flat, emotionless. But she could read things into what he'd said. As a home, it sucked. Probably hot in summer, cold in winter. And the kids at school would've given him hell for it. It was natural that he'd want it gone. But that didn't account for the pale grimness she'd seen on his face when he'd been forced to go inside.

And now she really wanted to stay. *Ugh.* Imogen got up.

"Where are you going?"

"Your room."

"Imm, I'm not going to strangle you in your sleep. One night isn't a proposal." His eyes were still closed, but his words were clear and even. Not angry. At least, not yet.

"I don't do spending the night," she blurted out, now hopelessly awake and cranky. "I don't want you here." Lies, lies, lies.

He grunted and let go of her wrist. Rolling to a seated position, he rubbed his face and got ready to rise. "If you're going back on your offer to let me stay if I told you about the bus, then I'm not leaving until I get something in return."

"You had fantastic sex..."

"To borrow your words, it's just sex." He grabbed his boxers and pulled them on as he stood, then made for the jeans. Now who was lying? "What's wrong with me spending a couple more hours sleeping beside you? Did someone once do something to you while you slept?"

"No," Imogen said, and was tempted to leave it there, but the sooner she told him, the sooner he'd leave. He claimed. "I don't do sleepovers because it's too close. I don't want to get that close. Because I'm going to leave. Feelings are born in sleeping together and shared mornings. And I don't want it to hurt when I have to leave again."

* * *

Wyatt watched her, the defiant way she held her head at odds with the way her arms wrapped around her middle, comforting herself. Protecting herself. Someone really had hurt her. If he tried to hug her now, she wouldn't thank him for it.

"You don't always have to leave. You're free-spirited so what's wrong with figuring it out as you go?" He didn't put his shirt or shoes on yet, waiting for her answer. And that hadn't been the right thing to say.

As much as he liked her, the temporary nature of their fling was the main reason it was okay. But maybe he could convince her to stick around for Amanda, not him. She didn't want anything permanent from him any more than he did, but he couldn't believe she liked this life on the road, no matter what she said.

"I have to stick to my schedule precisely because I'm impulsive and free-spirited. If I play it by ear, that leaves the possibility that I could stay, and I can't." She grabbed her robe and pulled it on, covering herself up.

"Because you tried to stay somewhere before?"

"Yes. Look, Wyatt, do you really want to do this now?" Imogen pulled her hair back from her face and headed for the sink, grabbing a washcloth and a tube of face stuff. She lathered and began furiously scrubbing away smeared makeup while answering his question. "Yes. I tried to settle down once, and it didn't work out. It went very badly, actually. I tried to stick with it, but after a few months I had to call my parents and have them come halfway across the country to help me get out. Out of a bad situation that I'd gotten myself into. Happy?"

"Settle down? You mean marriage?"

"Engaged. Living together. I got out before I had to hurdle any altars." Imogen rinsed and patted her thoroughly pink face dry with a towel.

She'd loved someone enough to settle down once. But the phrase that kept circulating through his mind was *"It went very badly."* He didn't know what to say. Genuine wariness shone in her eyes. The knowledge that some part of him frightened her didn't sit well. He grabbed his shirt and shoes then held out one arm. "Is a good-night kiss off the table?"

It took her a second, but she shook her head and stepped over to him. As his head descended, her eyes drifted closed. He held her a little more strongly than he might usually have, and kissed her until she leaned against him.

"I'm sorry I left you with Ed," Wyatt murmured against her lips, and actually meant it that time.

He didn't hang around long enough to get a response, just released her and padded barefoot through the door to his room and the cold bed awaiting him.

The rest of the week passed in a strange stalemate—Wyatt not asking about her ex, and Imogen not asking what about the bus upset him so much. They kept their separate rooms, but dined together nightly and enjoyed physical respite from the tension that burned through them by day. It never got more normal, more playful, less intense. But she never had to ask him to leave again. Imogen couldn't tell whether this was a healthy fling or not. Her whole view of life had skewed after that night. But a pattern of some sort was established, one Imogen hoped she could live with.

On Thursday evening they got Ole Shiny bus back on the road to head home.

Not home. To Amanda's house.

And on Friday Imogen assembled the crib she'd got for the baby and kept busy—cleaning, cooking and decorating Amanda's cottage for the coming week's baby shower, which she would miss.

On Saturday she found herself invited to the mountain for the first time, to help Wyatt with the cabin.

He gave his trust in pieces. But was she any different? Since she'd vigorously pointed out his nearly schizophrenic ability to change personalities, he'd been less prone to extremes. He was trying to integrate them, or at least gave the impression he was. But how long he could keep it up was what worried her. People didn't change overnight. And backsliding on a new lifestyle was the usual result.

Or she assumed those changes were because she'd pointed out the situation. Maybe he felt the odd tension too. It was enough at times that it was even hard for her to joke with and tease him.

The first part of the day she divided her time between actual work and actively trying not to look at or think about the old blue bus.

By the time they broke for lunch she couldn't contain her curiosity any longer. "Why did you put your practice on a bus?" The bus fixation needed to be explained.

Wyatt didn't answer immediately, like he had to

weigh the words for their worth before he could get them out. "When I was little, I was pretty ashamed of it." He tilted his head toward Ole Blue. "I asked my mamaw if I could come and live at her house. Amanda and Jolene's cottages were built for Mamaw and her mom. Jolene and my mom were sisters." He explained the family connection she'd never thought to ask about. Family that kept in touch. Land and homes that passed through the generations. Not something she was too familiar with.

"Anyway, she told me about a doctor who used to make rounds through the hills in his own bus when she was a girl. How good it was for the old folks and kids, everyone was in better shape when they were on his route." He paused to take another bite of his sandwich, finally letting himself look at the old bus. Talking about stuff, like anything else, Wyatt took at his own pace. The only time she'd seen the man in a hurry had been when he'd chased her.

"I think she was trying to help me see how finding a new job for an old vehicle could be a good thing. Took a while to sink in. But I guess it made an impression."

He was still ashamed of the blue bus, but he tried not to show it.

"I need to get rid of Dad's bus." He'd read her mind. "I don't like to go in there, but there are things that need to be sorted out before I can have it hauled away."

"Do you want—?" Imogen began.

"No," he cut in before she got the offer out. "I don't want anyone else doing it, Imm. I'll handle it."

"Is it a lot?"

"Not really. Pictures. Mom's jewelry box. Dad's crossbow." Wyatt made his way through a list, and muttered the last. "Josh's memory box."

The last was said so quietly she almost missed it.

"I'm the only one to survive that thing." His voice grew bitter and distant, and he stood, heading back to his chainsaw while she finished her sandwich.

What could she say to that? Somewhere in the back of her mind, since seeing the television and bed in there, she'd known it had been a home of some description. Not Wyatt's. He had a tent he stayed in when they weren't on the road, but the curtains and the television… It had clearly been a residence at some time. A very sad one. One she didn't know how to help him with.

She slumped on the log where she sat, forcing herself to finish eating. The day was only half-over, she'd need the fuel to keep up with Wyatt.

When the chainsaw roared to life, she was actually grateful to know he was engrossed in his task so he wouldn't see the tears that threatened.

The few words Wyatt had given her regarding the bus weren't a problem—much less had been said with many more syllables strung together. But the weight of all the words that had gone between them pressed Imogen into the mattress as she tried to sleep. Even getting comfortable was impossible.

It was about him and the bus and his brother and his dad. She didn't even know about how Wyatt's mom had died. Maybe he had been too little to really remember her?

The little boy who had begged his grandmother to let him live with her. The man who had bought the bus as temporary housing and had never left.

Every time she thought about it, she wanted to help Wyatt. Every time she wanted to help him, she came that much closer to the point where she'd consider staying. Just until he was better. Just until

Amanda was settled. Just until things changed, people changed, or maybe she changed. Just until they got tired of her.

Those were the thoughts that sent her crawling from bed three times in search of some sleep-inducing home remedy.

Book? Fail. Night-time headache pills? Double fail. Something full of carbs? Still no help.

At six a.m. Imogen crawled out of bed, not sure whether she'd actually slept at any point during the night.

She was supposed to go to the mountain again today.

Things to do before she went:

Shower.

Keep busy.

Don't think about the bus, the boy, the man, any of it.

Stay focused.

Ignore what he'd told her.

Why had she asked any of that? People didn't hold so tightly to meaningless secrets. She was a pusher, just like he'd said.

A pusher with sad, dry hair that needed some extra conditioning time. A half-hour in a towel was an absolute necessity. Which gave her just enough time to drink a measly pot of coffee to stay awake.

Breakfast. She'd declared she'd bring breakfast. Mountainside eating demanded something portable. Too bad he didn't have a landline hooked up. Maybe the bus had one. No, that was silly.

Who puts a phone in a bus?

"Someone who lives in a bus." Imogen sighed.

Don't think about the bus.

Buttermilk biscuits. She'd never made them, but Amanda had that instant breakfast flour that claimed you could make anything with it. The box had pictures of biscuits. No problem. She would bake her first batch of biscuits.

And when they were awful, she made her second batch.

He couldn't complain.

"Can't make biscuits on a bus."

She sighed and put them into the oven.

It had been a couple of days since she'd checked her emails so she should probably do that, just in case something important had happened.

And he said it might rain today so she'd better check the weather forecast.

Then there was that calendar she hadn't updated since she'd come here. She'd always kept track of exciting nationwide events she might like to attend—it made new hometown shopping easier when the time came. New River Gorge Bridge Day in West Virginia was in October.

Did Wyatt ever go to that?

"Of course he didn't go to that, stupid. He was away for decades because his life was a mess and everybody died." Imogen shut her laptop and trekked to the kitchen.

After the second batch of the biscuits came out of the oven, she cooked some sausages to death, splattering grease on her favorite PJs in the process. Now she had to do a load of laundry. It was important. Stuff she just had to do. Not just procrastination…

She crammed the food into the oven—food-safe heat—and went to get ready.

It was now just before eight. What did you wear to set logs? She sorted through her clothes, tested the material for strength and airiness, dressed and undressed, and examined her underwear.

Log-setting was probably the kind of thing they made those eighteen-hour bras for. But all the bras she owned were insubstantial, just like he'd called her that day on the mountain. Cute, but insubstantial and unreliable.

Unreliable, like someone who came late with an awful breakfast. And what must he think about her tardiness? Insubstantial was just another way to say stupid. Airhead. Blonde.

Imogen pressed her palms to her eyes. When she pulled them away everything looked blurry and wrong. Including the fuzzy red letters of the alarm clock.

After nine? It couldn't be that late yet. She went to check other clocks. Not that she could leave yet anyway. Her clothes weren't dry and they'd smell sour if she left them wet in the dryer all day. And should she leave the dryer running when she left? That was the kind of irresponsible thing someone unreliable did and got other people's houses burned down. Amanda's house was more important than her wrinkled pajamas.

Wyatt would just have to understand. If he was worried, he'd have been there by now. He wasn't worried. He was doing what he always did: playing with his big-boy building logs on the mountain while not looking at the bus.

Stop thinking about the bus.

She changed clothes again, putting her bikini on underneath. She didn't want to risk her pretty, insubstantial underwear, and didn't have time to get industrial-strength undergarments.

Just before ten she heard a knock on the door. Wyatt. She stalked to the door.

"Did I get stood up?" He didn't look angry, but it could be that he'd just misplaced his angry mask.

"You didn't get stood up." She had intended on going over. Sort of. But giving him an extra-special view into the chaos that qualified as her mind for the past twelve hours was out of the question. "I'm just running late. Breakfast's in the oven. Don't know how good it is."

Needing space, she left him to enter and jogged to the kitchen. *Keep moving, just keep moving.*

"The house looks great." He stepped in and looked over all the decorations she'd spent Friday hanging and the crib wrapped in a massive yellow, gender-neutral bow. "Everything okay?"

Lie. Lie or everything would get worse. "I'm fine. Restless night. Hard time getting going this morning."

"You don't have to come if you're tired, Imm. We could hold off if it'd be better for you." He had already been working, and he smelled like the forest and a little bit of sweat. Good God, if a parfumier could bottle that man…

"No, I'm good now. I'm ready and energized and I had a whole pot of coffee so I have been caffeine supercharged. Want jelly?"

"Sorry?"

"For the biscuits without sausage. They might be..."

He took a bite and immediately reached for the coffee she'd placed in front of him.

"Dry," she finished.

He grinned, but there was no way to even attempt talking until he'd cleared the sausage-flavored Styrofoam from his mouth.

"First biscuits?"

"Second." Her first day attempting to make them, but she left that part out. Today she needed to be normal. Fully tarted up in freshly laundered sanity without even an inch of her crazy slip showing.

With the help of milk, she choked down a biscuit too and turned off the dryer to leave.

"Hey." Wyatt hooked an arm around her waist as Imogen bustled for the door, stopping her effectively and anchoring her to him in the same motion. "I want you to know how much I appreciate your help with the cabin. I'm surprised you're not too sick of me by now to do it."

Please, don't bring up the talk, she silently pleaded, looking up at him. "I like your mountain and it gets dull watching Amanda lie in bed and read parenting books."

"Even if I win by default, I appreciate it." His arm loosened as he leaned down and brushed her lips with his. Kissing far surpassed talking in Imogen's list of things to do today. She turned to face him and leaned in, comforting herself with the feeling of his sturdy frame and warmth.

Wyatt took the hint and deepened his kiss, his tongue slipping into her mouth to stroke hers, arms winding around her. Happy to follow his lead, she let him take her as far as he wanted. No worries about his heart or hers, no weapons, just the heat and comfort of someone who wanted her around for the short time she'd be staying.

One of his arms tightened at her waist while the other slid down, anchored across the back of her thighs and lifted, curling her into his arms, so her feet were off the floor. Most men didn't pick Imogen up as she rivaled the height of most men she met, but Wyatt wasn't most men. The gentleness with which he laid her on the rug surprised her, as did his sudden interest in removing her clothes.

"I thought we were working today," she murmured, watching his strong hands unfasten and pull her shorts and panties off in one smooth motion.

"Later."

She nodded and toed her shoes off, her hands going to her shirt to pull it over her head. And then she noticed he wasn't taking his clothes off. He waited for her to be done and crawled between her legs. She realized what he was up to a second before his mouth began to play at her sex. Kissing. Licking. Slingshotting her from a tired, emotional wreck to a needy wanton in a matter of seconds. The best cure for emotional intimacy problems: physical intimacy.

Before long, his pants came off and he slid into her, somehow filling that hollow in her chest she'd been nursing since yesterday.

Whatever was wrong, Wyatt would fix it, one day at a time. Soon she'd be gone, and he'd forgive her. Move on. Make a life in something real she'd helped build. Proof she'd existed. One day, years from now, maybe he'd tell his grandkids the story of the cabin and remember the strange woman who had come to town and helped him build it.

October came and it was like Mother Nature flipped a switch. Kentucky might be part of the

South, but in the mountains at night the temperatures fell, and even during the hottest days temperatures never got high enough in the shade of the forest to feel truly warm.

Amanda's due date approached rapidly, and Imogen spent as much time on Jolene's couch as in Amanda's house. If Wyatt needed to come inside, she'd just have to find the strength to spend all her nights there.

When they were traveling, they maintained separate rooms. No matter how frequently they came together, neither of them ever spent the night in the other's bed. Sometimes they were in his room and she left, sometimes the other way around.

His mood, not especially light since he'd shown up at the bus that morning, only darkened as they drove down the winding roads toward the first town she'd visited with him in July, making this the beginning of her third lap around his patient route.

It soon became clear that ignoring his mood wouldn't help. What wasn't clear, though, was what had caused it. Maybe she could talk him out of it.

"Autumn in the Appalachians." She smiled over at him, intent on staying awake to figure out whatever had him in a lather. Sneakily figure him out.

The fastest way to increase his agitation was to ask directly what was wrong with the world's most secretive man. "I always intended on getting here for the foliage change. Maybe taking that old tourist train ride to see the leaves. Have you ever—?"

"You don't need to take a train to see the foliage," Wyatt cut in before she could get the question fully formed. "Just climb the mountain. Better view there than you'll get from a window on a train."

The man loved his mountain, but, having seen the view when the world had been green, Imogen was inclined to believe he meant it. Unfortunately, reminding him of the mountain didn't do anything for his mood. Next topic. "What about New River Gorge Bridge Day? That's coming up. How about we go?"

"You going to jump?" He looked over, brow up, the disproving frown she heard in his voice ready to form.

"Maybe. I'd like to." It was one of the few things West Virginia was famous for: base jumping from a massively high bridge spanning mountains. As far as she knew, no one had ever died during the Bridge Day festivities.

He shook his head.

She could feel the argument brewing behind his pursed lips. He wasn't Scott, but in that moment there was a tone in his voice that sent prickles up her spine and over the back of her head. Fear. Ridiculous. If she wanted to jump, he couldn't stop her. Suddenly his mood felt less important than pointing out to him that she knew what he was up to. "You don't want me to go."

"It's dangerous and pointless," Wyatt answered, not quite shouting but talking very loudly—much louder than the cab of the bus needed.

The near-shouting ratcheted up her agitation, near to rivaling his. It couldn't have been fear. Fear had always kept her from standing up to Scott, something that never happened with Wyatt. "So is chainsawing alone in the woods with no cell reception."

"No. That has a point," Wyatt muttered, his eyes still on the road, though narrowed now, not an expression she'd expect for arguing about small issues.

"So does jumping."

"No, it doesn't. There is no purpose to jumping off a bridge."

"Maybe no practical purpose, but there is a purpose." He'd been spoiling for a fight the whole time. Whatever she said, it would just be ammunition for him to build whatever argument suited him.

"Enlighten me." Wyatt glanced at her, only for a second before he focused again on the road but it was enough to estimate his feelings about free falling.

"This is stupid."

"At last we agree. So you aren't going to go jump off a bridge."

Imogen turned to look at him, squinting. "You seriously don't know me at all if you think forbidding me from doing something isn't going to make me do it faster. You want to know why I want to? A test of bravery. Because you have to learn to control fear so it doesn't paralyze you." She looked away again. Let him sit there flexing his jaw and bunching his angry eyebrows until it made his otherwise handsome profile look Neanderthal.

"Falling that far should scare you. It could kill you." Smug. God, she hated this Smug Doctor mask.

"Go ahead, say you wouldn't let me do it." She didn't need to look at him. The world zooming past her window was a lot more peaceful, even at sixty miles per hour.

"I can't stop you from doing anything you have a mind to do, Imogen. I doubt even you can stop yourself from doing things you shouldn't do. I'm starting to see the best I can do is damage control. You do what you want, when you want." Wyatt reached over and turned on the radio.

Imogen turned it right off again. "What damage control have you been doing on me? The last I checked, I'm the one doing damage control on you."

Wyatt turned the radio back on again.

She really was going to hurt him. "When you figure out what's bothering you, let me know so I can get to work fixing it."

CHAPTER NINE

"EMMA-GEE, Emma-Gee, Emma-Gee…"

Imogen knew that voice. She turned to look over her shoulder as the Petersons entered, Michael chanting her name. "Emily, Brandon. Hi. And look at Michael! No more cast!" She reached for the toddler, giving Emily some respite from carrying him. "How's he been?"

"No more itching," Emily announced. "Can't keep that splint on him, though. He knows how to rip the Velcro straps and get it off."

"He's doing that a lot?" Imogen smiled at Brandon and led them to an exam room.

"He used to always rip his clothes off, left and right, and all that focus is on the splint now. Take your eyes off him, and off it comes."

"Dr. Beechum, the Petersons are here." Imogen popped her head into the other exam room where Wyatt sat with his tablet.

"Be right there." Distracted. Working on files or working on avoiding her. After the quarrel in the bus on Monday, they'd spent their first evening apart while on the road. They hadn't even eaten together but had taken their delivered meals to their own rooms. Imogen sulked and tried not to think about what she was feeling.

She deposited Michael on the table and took his vitals. As Wyatt walked in, she freed the scrawny little arm from the splint, much to Michael's delight.

Imogen moved out of the way, leaving the little wriggler with Wyatt and Emily to go and lean by Brandon, who was doing his best to be as thirteen as possible. So surly.

"Hates that splint, eh? They have him doing physical therapy?" Wyatt turned around and dug in one of the drawers, from which he produced a small rubber bone that he removed from packaging. When had he picked that up? Was that a dog toy?

"Yeah, there's a bunch of exercises I'm supposed to try and get him to do, but he doesn't want to." Emily watched what Wyatt was doing, a small frown on her face.

"I know this looks weird, and the noise will drive you nuts, but the rubber is the softest I could find and I figure the squeaking will keep him interested for a while to keep him working the arm." A pause and he handed the bone to Michael in such a way that the toddler took it with his injured arm. Wyatt gave it a squeeze. Michael laughed and then began squeezing it incessantly.

"He's using both hands," Emily pointed out.

"That's okay," Wyatt said, petting the little guy's head and raising his voice enough to be heard over the din. "He's using it, and that's the point. The more he uses it, the stronger he'll get. But too much right away will overtire him. Give it to him a couple of times a day to start, and then a few times a day, and by the time he's starting to get bored with it, he'll be using the arm for other stuff. And you can bin the noisemaker."

Doctor Face was nowhere in sight. And Imogen found herself smiling at Wyatt, totally wrecking her surly wall-lean with Brandon.

He smiled back, the first smile this week. Her breathing hitched a little. Silly to get emotional about that, he just had such a great smile.

"How are the seizures?" When Michael started squeezing with only his good hand, Wyatt casually swapped the bone to the other hand and picked Michael up so the good arm was over his shoulder and out of sight.

"Still having them. We are going to the other

doctor next week, but he's going to ask about the medicine and I don't know what to tell him. I don't feel like they're getting much of a shot to work because we have such a hard time getting them in him regular."

"Tried crushing them and putting them in something?" Wyatt asked.

"He can taste it and he's gotten wise to the trick," Emily murmured.

"A reward system might work. I hate to say give him candy when he does it, but you could follow the daily dose with one or two chocolates or chewy sweets. A very low amount, just until you get the habit formed," Wyatt said, looking at The Mad Squeaker for a moment then back at Emily. "Got to find a way to keep them in him. Don't want you bashing any other limbs, do we, buddy?"

Michael squeaked the toy. He wasn't paying attention to Wyatt.

Brandon looked down and sighed. Imogen might not have noticed it if she hadn't been leaning right beside him.

Wyatt noticed it too. He looked at the boy with a sharpness that made the hair on Imogen's neck stand on end, but she didn't exactly understand why.

Brandon obviously interpreted it as his cue to leave. He mumbled something and stepped out of the room, just as he had on their last visit.

"Brandon was supposed to be watching Michael when he fell, but he was paying more attention to his video game than his brother." Emily shook her head. It was easy to see that she held her elder son responsible for the injury of the younger.

Wyatt focused on the woman, his brows pinching as he gently handed her youngest back to her. Michael dropped his toy.

Emily's words made Imogen feel uncomfortable, and as she bent forward to retrieve the toy she tried to summon words to champion the older boy. "Accidents happen." Okay, so what came out was lame. A platitude. Like that would help anyone. But the subject was touchy. No one would want to dive into this conflict.

"I hope you haven't been saying that to Brandon. I'm sure he's saying it to himself enough on his own, without you adding to the guilt he feels." Okay, so maybe Wyatt didn't mind diving into that conflict. "Did you see what he'd written on Michael's cast?"

"He needs to understand how important it is to watch Michael." She didn't answer the question.

"Yes. And you're his mother. You're Michael's mother, and you're Brandon's mother. At the end of the day, Michael's welfare is your responsibility, not a twelve-year-old boy's."

Michael screamed and strained for the toy, which Imogen handed back to him, replacing the scream with more squeaking.

Wyatt's rule was not to question his calls in front of patients. But he was wound tighter than she'd ever seen him. And Emily was on the verge of tears.

"How about I go talk to Brandon? I'll tell him—"

Wyatt's look silenced her. *Dangerous.*

"Nothing that boy could've done would've gotten him to Michael in time for him to be moved to the floor. And picking up a thrashing child is hard enough for an adult." He chewed on nothing again, the corner of his jaw working overtime. Holding back from saying something worse?

Emily said nothing. Her eyes sparkled and she swayed, comforting the child who couldn't be distracted from his squeaky toy enough to notice his mommy was about to cry.

"Get the medicine in him if you want him safe. Any questions?"

Imogen couldn't speak. She stood frozen, it was the only way to keep from running out of there.

Emily shook her head.

Wyatt took a deep breath, put his hand gently over Michael's head, and stepped out.

Doctor Face would've been better than Angry Doctor Face.

Imogen leaned off the wall and went to make a little fuss over Michael and Emily, doing her best to take attention away from Wyatt's words and his exit. Yes, it had probably needed to be said, but there were gentler ways to say things. If you weren't furious…

"Let's get that splint back on. I'm going to send this roll of athletic tape with you. If he refuses to keep the splint on, give it a couple wraps with the tape over the Velcro straps. It will get a bit sticky when the tape is removed, but it'll make it harder for him to get it off."

Talking. Talking in a helpful tone and saying things, anything, would help. Imogen babbled, spewing her best advice. "The other thing you could try is to get a small sock, like something that Brandon wore a few years ago? Cut the toes out and a hole for the thumb, and just slide that over the splint so his fingers come out the holes like a sheath. Out of sight, out of mind. Maybe he'll forget about the straps and the fun noises they make if he doesn't see them."

She took extra time, getting some snuggles with Michael before they exited with their oddly endearing puppy chew toy/physical therapy aid.

Imogen stepped out behind them to head for their waiting area and sign-in sheet. She should give Wyatt a few minutes to compose himself before she called the next patient.

He was a man at war with himself. On one hand was the caring man who, between visits, had actively gone out and searched stores for something to help with Michael's injury. And on the other hand the angry man who yelled at the mother of young patients.

"It'll be just a few minutes," Imogen announced to the last couple of patients waiting to be seen. She went back inside to check on Wyatt.

"Hey," she said softly to his back where he stood, bent over a counter, making notes in the files.

"Give me five minutes and I'll be ready for the next patient." His voice was level. Cold. She had at least expected anger, or to be told to mind her own business.

"But are you okay? Do you want—?"

"I don't want to talk about it. I said my piece to Mrs. Peterson."

Emily. He had brought the woman back down to formal titles. Distancing himself.

Imogen stepped into the exam room to make sure it was tidy and ready for the next patient.

Imogen stood outside the rental office, breathing the clean mountain air deeply while Wyatt handled the room transaction with the innkeeper. She glanced through the window, checking on his progress, and rather than a smiling woman and Charming Face, they both looked dour. His mood was so bad.

Since Michael's visit that afternoon, his mood had gotten worse and worse. At least, that's how it seemed. He'd got more and more distant. Colder. So at odds with the image he'd been working to present to the patients.

He stalked to the door so quickly she barely had time to move to avoid being plowed out of the way. She held her hand out for her room key, the usual manner in which this exchange happened, and Wyatt simply took her by the hand and pulled her along to his usual room.

"Wyatt?"

"We're sharing a room," he said, opening the door and dragging her in with him.

Something in the way he moved held her tongue. She walked into the room and sat down on one of the beds, her gaze focused on him. He'd taken a strange position against the door, both palms braced against it, leaning with his head down. Anger, tension and sadness. He had brought her there for a reason, and Imogen couldn't face the idea of making him talk. Not yet.

Carefully, Imogen stood, removed her jacket and walked over to him. Ducking under one arm, she slid between his body and the door and lifted her hands to cradle his cheeks. His eyes were still shuttered to her. These masks of his were going to be the death of her.

After his regression today, faith was in short supply. But she still wanted to comfort him. Give him some relief. Leaning in, she kissed him, dragging him with her into the desire they both knew so well and away, she prayed, from emotions he never wanted to talk about. When he responded, his kiss was raw and primitive. All need. Almost feral.

Her hands fell to his belt and began tearing at the closure, unfastening it as fast as she could. Her scrubs were easier to remove, but she managed to get his pants down and his shirt open before they hit the bed.

He pulled her onto him, an oasis of pleasure or temporary forgetfulness. But the look in his eyes, behind the dark need, was pain. It was almost worse than being shut out from them.

She took him into her and rode him hard. The hands that had always touched her gently squeezed her hips with nearly bruising desperation. This was supposed to make them both feel better, but his eyes told a different story. One echoed by the sob she choked back.

His climax hit hard, jerking his body with such force he nearly toppled her. And she didn't reach hers with him. That was a first. But her emotions were too raw and too tied to the turmoil she saw bubbling beneath the surface.

Shaky, she lay against him, tucking her nose under his jaw and resting one arm on the pillow beside his head to comb her fingers through his hair until he stopped trembling. Until they both stopped trembling.

When his breathing slowed, his body relaxed and she lifted her head to look down at him.

"I handled that wrong. With Emily." Wyatt spoke first, his voice quiet.

He needed to talk about it. The shutters were gone, but sadness lingered. If she was going to let him get it out without crying for him, she couldn't look him in the eye. "What did Brandon write on Michael's cast?" she whispered, and laid her head back down, her nose right there in the nook where the short, crisp beard faded to bare skin on his neck. Safe.

"He wrote, 'I'm sorry,'" Wyatt mumbled. "Drew a heart. He comes with them because he wants to know what is going on with his brother. He wants the truth, not what his parents decide to tell him. But he always leaves because he feels so much guilt."

It sounded like he spoke from experience. Mr. Shoemaker's words came back to her: *It wasn't right for your daddy to put all that on you.*

"When people care for children who become ill, it's very common for them to blame themselves." She kept petting his hair, feeling the silky black strands slip through her fingers. "It's a lot worse when that illness is serious. Guilt can eat you alive. Strip away everything."

"Brandon didn't cause that seizure. Someone needs to say that to him. It should be his mother, but I don't think she's going to." A remnant of anger tinged his words, but there was no heat behind them right now. The day had exhausted them both. "They strike so fast. He probably couldn't have kept Michael from falling even if he had been holding the boy when the seizure hit."

He still thought that she was only talking about the Peterson boys.

Or he was ignoring the subtext.

"And sometimes people with seriously ill children blame others," Imogen added softly, tilting her head so she could look him in the eye again.

He wasn't ready to talk about that part. Which was probably good. He'd heard her, that's all she needed. Soul-baring conversations…how did they keep coming up with this man? "You want to go back and talk to them?" It seemed unlikely he'd feel better about this until he did something about it.

"Tomorrow. After our other stop. Before heading home. Brandon should be home from school then."

"House call?" Imogen perked up, smiling weakly. Her first house call.

Wyatt nodded. "I'll sit them down."

"No." She waved a hand quickly. "You talk to Brandon. I'll talk to Emily. If you put them together, they'll both go on the defensive. And after the way things went with Emily..."

He looked doubtfully at her. "You up for giving it to her straight?"

"I'm up for it," Imogen said. "Are you up for keeping scary Doctor Face away?"

"I'm not going to yell at anyone."

She shifted on him, rising up to kiss him. She'd been wanting to do that all day. "The doggy toy. That was inspired. Wonderful."

Wonderful and scary. If that face, the New Improved Face she glimpsed before Scary Doctor came back... If he asked her to stay...

Not just for one night. Stay. For real. She'd be tempted. She was tempted, even with him teetering on the verge of crazy today.

Just for tonight she could stay with him. She knew he wanted it. They both wanted it. Stupid. One night wouldn't make them emotionally entangled. They were already entangled. Or at least she was. Knotted and twisted. It could all end up like it had with Scott. But that took more than one night. Probably.

"Do you still love the farmer?" Wyatt asked. "I don't know his name."

How did he do that? Picking through her thoughts like he had a direct line.

"No," Imogen said softly, still combing her fingers through the black hair at his temple. "Whatever love I felt for Scott, he made sure it died."

"What did he do to you?" His voice was little more than a whisper.

It really wasn't fair of her to expect him to talk about his hurts if she refused to do the same. "He..." She hated talking about Scott so much it was hard to even make her mind select words. "He made everyone think he was someone good. Someone different." She stumbled her way through.

"Did he hit you?"

"Not really." Imogen had to fight the urge to pull away from Wyatt. He must have felt it as his arms tightened around her.

"How do you not really hit someone?" Wyatt's arms contracted, squeezing her a little tighter.

"Shoves. Grabs. Shakes."

"What else?"

"At first he was just very angry. Said things. About me. But he was different in public. With his parents. With our friends," Imogen murmured, sighing. "I never knew what version of Scott I'd be dealing with."

"What things did he say?" Wyatt's hand was moving now, stroking her back as she played with his hair.

"Does it matter?"

"Yes," he whispered.

"He called me names. Said I was stupid. Accused me of things. Cheating." She kept her nose tucked against the side of his neck, but she couldn't keep away the tension that blew through her when she talked about Scott. "He didn't think much of me. I don't want to talk about this anymore."

"Will you stay tonight?" Wyatt asked. "If you want me to, I can go and get the other room. I have another key."

Her choice. And she wanted to stay.

"I'll stay. Just no more talking about bad stuff," Imogen whispered. Dealing with old wounds on the first night she stayed with him? Too much at once.

"No more talking about bad stuff," Wyatt agreed.

She closed her eyes and released a slow breath, turning her head so her cheek was pillowed on his chest.

Nothing would change because she stayed.

One night wasn't that big a deal.

* * *

Slam the door in Wyatt's face. That's what Imogen would do if she were Emily and Wyatt came knocking the day after basically calling her a bad mother.

The rain had been coming down hard since yesterday, and she half expected the access road to Bent Reed to be blocked. As it was, the creek had yet to top the bridge.

Wyatt stopped the bus at the top of the road and surveyed the creek, as far up and down the stream as he could see through the trees on the bank. "We probably have a couple of hours before it gets impassable," he murmured, looking at Imogen. "Keep an eye on the clock, okay?"

"Okay." If worse came to worst, they had snacks and uncomfortable vinyl exam tables they could lie on for a couple of hours while the water receded.

Wyatt carefully navigated the bus down the incline from the highway and then to the bridge and over it. The water was still a couple of feet away from the bottom of the bridge. They'd be okay. Everything would be okay. They just had to get in and out quickly.

Wyatt knew where the Petersons lived, and pulled up in front of their house. Imogen got up and grabbed her jacket and umbrella. "I'll send Brandon out if I can talk Emily into it. If not, I will talk to Brandon."

"Tell her I will come apologize if you need to." Not that it sounded like he wanted to apologize to Emily. Emily was at the top of his Angry Face list right now.

"I will." Imogen dashed out, sticking to the stepping stones that led across the yard and changing the angle of the umbrella to keep out of the rain.

Emily answered the door. "Imogen." She looked past her to the bus and frowned. "What can I do for you?"

"I'd like to talk to you about what happened yesterday. And Wyatt would really like to speak with Brandon." When Emily didn't say anything, Imogen added, "He wants to make things right, Emily. There's some things about Wyatt's family that you need to know."

The woman considered for a moment and then opened the door, letting Imogen in. After handing her umbrella to Brandon, she took a seat on a wooden chair, very aware of her wet clothes.

Brandon stepped out and Imogen began. "Wyatt wouldn't thank me for telling you this but I think you need to understand why he reacted the way he did yesterday. Wyatt's little brother died when Wyatt was a child..."

Wyatt sat on a rolling stool in the lobby area of the bus, waiting for the hangman's noose. Or for the door to open, and for either Brandon to step aboard, as requested, or for Imogen to return with the news that he'd wrecked the name of his practice in this neck of the woods.

Funny how he'd been so dead set against her working for him, and now the fate of his practice might be in the delicate hands of the ballsy outsider who'd stormed his mountain and demanded a job.

She'd probably win Emily over in the same fashion. Demand the woman listen to her. Demand she stop blaming the boy for his brother's injury. Demand she forgive *him* for his sharp words.

The door opened and to his relief Brandon stepped in, then closed the door and his umbrella before he looked at Wyatt. Brandon was a patient, but if Wyatt had learned nothing else from the past few weeks, and from yesterday especially, he couldn't treat him as a patient today.

Wyatt stood and stepped forward, offering his hand, which Brandon shook tentatively.

"Thank you for coming to talk to me. Pop?"

Wyatt gestured to the different cans of soda on the counter.

"Sure. Thanks." The boy took one and sat, waiting like he expected to be yelled at.

Wyatt knew that look. You could get survivor's guilt when no one had died yet. "I'm not here as your doctor or as Michael's doctor. I just want to talk to you man to man." Man to boy sounded condescending.

"There are some things you need to know about your little brother's illness. But the most important one is this: when the seizures come, they hit like flood waters. You can't stop them. Michael fell. Even if you'd been holding him, there's only a tiny chance that you'd have been able to hold him. He would've fallen no matter what you did. It's not your fault."

The kid sat there for long seconds, his knees starting to bounce. Agitated. Nervous. Guilty. "If he was on the floor with me," he said after a minute, "he wouldn't have fallen."

"He's two. He's starting to notice the difference between what big boys do and what little boys do. He wants to be like you."

"He says he's a big boy all the time."

"Big boys sit on the couch," Wyatt said softly.

"Your mom is having a hard time with the epilepsy. You're going to have to ignore it if she says those kinds of things again. She's trying to deal with it, and she's scared about what might happen. She'll get past it, and it's most likely that Michael will grow out of these seizures when he gets older. But you can't control everything life throws at you. Sometimes the best you can do is damage control." And preventative care. Wyatt frowned for a moment as the kid sat, nodding and drinking his pop. "Brandon, how much does he follow you around?"

"All the time. Dad calls him my ditto."

"I've just had an idea how you could help get your family some control back on the seizures. Do you take vitamins?"

"Vitamins? Not usually."

Wyatt stood and made a quick trip to the pharmacy case. When he came back he handed Brandon a bottle of Vitamin C pills. "This is your medicine that the doctor gave you. Michael has his and you have yours. When it's time for his medicine, have your mom fix up your pills first. How does she do it?"

"Crushes them and puts in apple sauce."

"Have her crush one of these for you, put it in

apple sauce, and show Michael that you're taking your medicine too. Big boys take their medicine." Wyatt sat back down, keeping himself more or less on eye level with Brandon. Not intimidating doctor. Just a dude.

"Vitamin C is sour enough to cave your mouth in, so you'll probably want a drink afterwards. But if you can, use that sourness. Make it funny. Make a terrible face. Shake. Be dramatic. Make him laugh. And then when he's done laughing at you, tell him it's his turn. If he likes to mimic you, like he seems to…"

Brandon smiled, looking at the bottle but clearly imagining the scene and how it would play out. And feeling like he could really help his brother.

"Think you can handle it? Those suckers are seriously sour." Wyatt grinned in return, feeling warm all over, despite the cold rainy day.

He hoped Imogen was getting on as well with Emily.

Sometime while Imogen was talking with Emily, the sky opened up and already hard rain was falling in such quantity that she couldn't see the bus from the front window of the Petersons' house. She waited until Brandon returned with her umbrella—he was soaked even using it. And getting out there fast wouldn't help them get out of Bent Reed any faster. No one could drive in this kind of visibility.

She ran with the umbrella shielding her, and when she got into the bus she was as wet as Brandon had been. "He looked happy. How was it?"

Shaking the umbrella at the door, she closed it and stashed it so she could come inside.

"Don't think it could have gone better." Wyatt smiled at her, but when she stepped forward to hug him he shrugged back.

Her shoes made squishy sounds as she walked. That should've told her how wet she was. That, and how cold she was.

"We might be here awhile so maybe we should get you out of those wet clothes."

Imogen laughed. He must be feeling better. "Don't you want to know how it went with Emily?"

"Right now I'm feeling too good to ask."

"I told her some things so she'd understand your reaction."

He paused and looked at her for longer than was comfortable.

"I don't know that much, so I couldn't say too

much." Her mouth twisted and she considered going back to the Petersons'.

"Did it work?" His voice was quiet.

"I think so." She waited.

Wyatt nodded, and his shoulders seemed to relax a bit. "Let's get you dry before you freeze." He stepped around her to lock the door and they adjourned to one of the exam rooms. Good thing they had an overnight bag. And condoms.

Half an hour later the rain hadn't let up much. Imogen could tell from the roar of it hitting the top of the bus. But pounding on the main door indicated that someone else was brave enough to get out in it. Wyatt straightened his clothes first and stepped out, closing the door behind him so Imogen could have privacy to dress.

She heard the muffled sounds of greeting and stepped out in time to see a drenched man standing just inside the bus say, "My wife sent me to fetch you two in. Don't look like you're going to get out of here anytime soon, thought you might like to come see the news and weather."

Wyatt looked out the window and then back at the drenched man. "I appreciate the offer, Nate. In the damp and cold, even this modern bus gets chilly. We'll wait a little bit to see if the rain slows up some."

Nate agreed and let himself back out. Wyatt turned to Imogen. "Looks like you patched things up with me with Emily." He wrapped his warm arms around her again.

She smiled to herself, hugging him back.

CHAPTER TEN

RUN-OFF FROM THE great hills channeled where two or more merged, concentrating the water into torrents. It had been more than twenty-four hours since the Petersons had taken them in. More than two hours since the rain had stopped, but the water seemed higher to Imogen now than when it had still been coming down.

Little Michael had been on her hip for most of her stay, and wasn't ready to get down yet—even now, asleep, she couldn't get away with it. Every time she tried to put him into his crib, the little monkey woke up and cried. As tiring as it was to cart him around, she appreciated having him in her arms to cuddle. The flooding spooked her.

In a nearby lot, where Wyatt had moved the bus after the rain had stopped, patches of dry-looking asphalt started appearing. On the blacktop near it, people gathered—a goodly portion of the small neighborhood, by the look of it. They had chairs, food and wood. By the time the bonfire roared to life, Emily came back to announce an impromptu wiener roast, and sent Brandon to find sticks.

"Want to go down?" Wyatt asked. "They're probably doing this because we're here." Staying with the Petersons had defined them as a couple. As far as most of the patients knew, they just worked together. Or maybe they were friends. But they were on decidedly different ground with this small family.

The funny thing was it didn't bother her that they regarded Wyatt and her as a couple.

"Looks like fun," Imogen added in a quieter voice, "and it's good for the practice. Great place for you to keep trying out your new and improved bedside manner."

Emily relieved her of the red-clad, toddler-shaped growth she'd sprouted, leaving her free to walk to the blacktop with Wyatt.

Once out the door, he slipped his hand into hers. The last hours had been the longest they'd gone without touching since they'd stopped fighting that attraction, and the hours since then made the rush of feeling so strong it nearly robbed her of breath. Imogen usually liked to leapfrog over hand-holding and get to the sexy stuff. But she wanted to touch Wyatt. His hand felt both foreign and familiar, comfortable and exciting.

It was strange, like heightened desperation followed by release. Not orgasmic. More like releasing a tether that stretched harder the further they were apart. Like moments after pain ended, and the relief was so acute it could bring tears.

She tried to focus on the gathering they approached, and fought the heat she felt around her eyes. She was feeling emotional. Way too emotional for a wiener roast.

Since their first kiss, the feeling was always there. She'd associated it with sex and desire, but right now she didn't feel particularly sexy, and it was still there. Stronger, maybe.

They sat at the fire and she wiggled free again, taking Michael back into her lap as everyone talked and roasted freshly skewered hot dogs on branches held over the fire.

As far as her experience with Appalachian potlucks went, this one won. There had been a kind of order and etiquette to the Grange potlucks with horseshoes and banjos, but here people just talked. Wyatt talked about his cabin construction with the men. Imogen talked travel with the women. Everyone had stories and no one minded that she wasn't from there. They all knew someone who drove a big truck and saw America in a blur of highways.

The surprising thing was that no one asked if or when she was going to leave—even after hearing the list of places she'd lived. They just assumed she was there to stay. As if it was incomprehensible she'd leave after being in these old mountains where economic lines didn't really matter and they weren't separated by occupation or family. They all bled moss and black earth, just like Wyatt.

What was worse, the conversation brought a revelation: she hadn't thought about her next town since the morning she'd delayed going to the mountain. Not a single daydream. Even the morning she'd freaked out, she'd only surfed the web for things to do in the area. Bridge Day. Looked at the Appalachian Trail hikes—which she'd since forgotten all about. She spent all her time working with Wyatt in some fashion, or visiting Amanda, and didn't even remember the world of things she wanted to do.

When her hot dog was ready, she handed Michael to his mom and ate in silence. Wyatt peppered her with inquisitive looks, but staying with the Petersons kept too much talking at bay.

And what could she say when he started asking

things again? *I love you but I can't stay here because this place is too rural and—*

Wait…

Love? She choked on her hot dog. Just enough to make everyone stare and Wyatt get that Heimlich gleam in his eye. With an effort she swallowed past it and got a drink to clear her throat. Everyone went back to talking.

She didn't want to love him. Insane attraction was okay. Concern for him and all the stuff he had to overcome with family issues was natural. She'd feel that for anyone whose history she'd been stupid enough to dig into.

The laughing and chatter around the fire returned to normal and then became very loud. She stood up. "I'm going to have a walk and see how far the water's come up the hill."

She didn't tell him because she loved him. It was just being polite.

"Everything okay?" His voice was quiet, not loud enough for anyone else to hear.

"I just need some space."

He nodded. She'd said this to him a few times since they'd met, when things got to be too much. "Don't go too far, please."

With the rest of her life-threatening hot dog in

hand, she walked the short distance to the top of the swell of land and stopped. The water was higher now. How could it still be rising? When they'd all gone to the bonfire it had been several feet further down the slope.

It had a sound. An oceanic roar, blended with destructive undertones—the sound of timber crashing together as it rushed along the swollen stream, a steel drum clanging into mostly submerged metal signs announcing there could be high water ahead.

Dangerous. This place was one of the most dangerous she'd ever worked. Maybe. It seemed like it. Sure, crime was rarer probably, and the only traffic she'd encountered had been tractors on the road, but there were floods and snakebites and accidental gunshots. Or maybe someone's head would explode. Her head certainly felt like she was developing a case of Appalachian Cranial Combustion.

And that would probably be better. It would certainly take the pressure off figuring out what she was supposed to do.

She knew what she wanted. Oh, she'd been denying it for a while, but through the whole night when she slept on the couch and Wyatt had slept protectively on the floor in front of her, she'd wanted nothing more than to climb down and sleep beside him.

The looming threat of Wyatt faces she hadn't yet seen kept her from making that leap. What if all the faces she loved were the masks and Angry Doctor was the real him?

What would be worse: leaving while it hurt, or waiting until they relaxed enough to really be themselves and having to leave when things got bad?

Because she did love him. She loved what he did, and why he did it. She even loved his accidental sexist slips and out-of-place chivalry—real or fake.

She forced down the last of the hot dog, and with it swallowed the last vestiges of hope. Amanda was near term now. Soon the baby would come, and she would have to face reality and make some decisions. As soon as she figured out what reality was.

Behind her, Wyatt yelled her name with an urgency that demanded she turn around. Before she turned, everyone started yelling her name. Her first glimpse of the group was a couple of dozen horrified faces and waving arms.

When Wyatt, Emily and Nate broke into a dead run for her, she realized who wasn't at the bonfire: Michael.

Spinning back toward the water, she saw a flash of red bobbing in the muddy waters. He was still close enough for her to swim to. She could reach him. She could do it…

The next thing she knew, she was tumbling with the racing current, fighting to keep her head above water and her eyes on the red-clad toddler bobbing through the torrent ahead of her.

Wyatt hurdled the log he'd been sharing with Imogen and tore across the lot to where she and the boy had disappeared. His heart in his throat, he frantically scanned the branch-infested edges of the swollen stream, hoping to find her there with the boy.

Nothing.

He heard footsteps behind him and the sound of Emily crying. Going in after Imogen felt like the right call, but he had to keep a cool head. Clear thinking first. Emotions would not help him find her. Throwing himself into the water where he'd have to save himself too wouldn't do any good for any of them.

He needed speed. Organizing the others would take too long. Wyatt ran along the top of the embankment, downstream, his eyes scanning the trees on both sides of the creek. He hadn't gone more than a few hundred feet before his path ended where another heavy channel of run-off joined the temporary river the creek had become.

Nate reached him as he searched the trees for a way to get over the water.

"It's too heavy, that rut is deeper than you think." Nate rubbed a hand over his face, walking in a small circle. "Someone went to call the squad. I don't know. I don't know what to do."

"Go back to your family." Wyatt looked up the hill and then back to the water. Climb to pass it, or go in? A flash of red? No white, not that her hoodie would still be white in that water, but if she saw the red, that's where she'd try to go.

Turning, he pounded back upstream, far enough that he could get into the creek and to the middle before that channel of run-off added to its power.

"Wyatt?"

There was no time to answer Nate's questions. Imogen was here because of him. He had taken her on. He'd screwed up badly enough they'd had to come back to Bent Reed. He'd taken the chance they could get back out before the flood waters rose too high and blocked the way. He'd let her wander toward the water and the bank had been at his back. If he'd sat facing the other way, he'd have seen the boy and stopped him before he got anywhere near Imogen and the water.

The sound of the water nearly deafened him. As he ran, he searched for areas to get through the trees to the water.

Her desire to help had trumped her attempts to control her impulses. Was she a strong swimmer? He'd learned not to discount her abilities in anything before letting her try. She was strong, and more stubborn than...

Please be more stubborn than the water!

He found a clearing on the bank and backed up to get a run at it.

The water was so cold his muscles immediately contracted and a log slammed into his side, knocking him under the water and spinning him around. When he got to the surface again, adrenaline had his arms and legs obeying. He got his breath and searched the bank ahead, doing all he could to stay facing forward.

Red. Caught in the trees on the opposite bank ahead. Why wasn't Michael still moving with the current? Was he caught on something? Tree?

He only saw glimpses as he fought the water spinning him round.

Something broke the surface behind Michael. A once white hood. Imogen's head.

With a deep breath he dove down and swam hard for the other side, swimming beneath the dangerous debris that floated on the surface. When he surfaced, he was a few trees up from them and had to hand-walk along the lower branches to get there.

She had one arm hooked around a branch and the other latched onto the back of Michael's coveralls.

"Imogen!" he yelled, hoping she could hear him over the water. "I'm coming!"

The toddler screamed. Good. He was still breathing. But by the time he got there, water had risen over Imogen's head.

Reaching the tree, he pulled himself onto a higher branch and anchored his legs around it, freeing his hands to reach for them both. At the first touch of his hand Imogen's hand spun and latched on to his fingers. He pulled her up. Her legs were under the water, providing another layer of support to keep Michael above the torrent.

"Help me, honey."

"Michael," Imogen gasped. "Save Michael."

"I aim to save you both," Wyatt grunted, grabbing her by the hoodie and the boy by the back of his bibs and pulling with all his might. "Climb, Imm. I have him. Get higher. I'll hand him to you."

Blood. The back of her hoodie had a stripe of blood on it. Get them from the water then check her injury. She was strong. She could still climb.

Michael screamed louder as Imogen released him and Wyatt started to lift the little guy free from the water.

Already his body was slowing down. Cold sapped strength fast, making everything harder.

The water still rose. They'd have a way to climb to reach safety. She straddled a branch above him and reached back for the boy. Wyatt handed him up, climbed above her and reached back for Michael. He did his best to help Imogen climb and then handed the child over again. In this fashion, they climbed to about ten feet above the stream.

Wyatt settled in a cradle of large, close-together branches and pulled them both into his cold, shaking arms.

Once everyone was settled, Wyatt started pulling at Imogen's hoodie, trying to get a look at her back.

"Check Michael first," she demanded.

With a muttered curse Wyatt gently pulled the little guy more into his arms than Imogen's and put his ear to the toddler's chest to try and hear any rattling from water he might have inhaled. Between the screaming and the roar of the water, what on earth did he expect to hear? Imogen's bleeding seemed the more acute injury, but she was damned stubborn about these things. "I can't hear anything in his lungs. Or any rattle in his crying."

Imogen started unfastening the boy's clothes, pulling aside the sopping material to check his body for signs of trauma. Wyatt joined her, and before long they had him stripped to his underpants and she shifted her attention to trying to calm him.

Her voice shook but he couldn't tell if it was from effort or fear. "It's okay, Michael. We've got you. And we'll get you warm."

Wyatt prodded gently at the toddler's belly and investigated a bruise forming on his back.

"Check his arm," Imogen directed.

"The splint protected it," Wyatt said, but still checked the other limbs and fingers. "Nothing's broken. Take off your jacket." He waited for the jacket to come off. She took the shirt off with it and then reached for the boy again, pulling him to her chest and wrapping her arms around him. Bare skin would be warmer than wet, cold clothes. Especially with the sun out.

He fixed his gaze on the five-inch gash crossing the left side of her back, angling down from below her shoulder blade toward her hip. "It's not a pretty cut, like mine was."

"Ruined for a bikini." Her teeth chattered, but Michael was crying a little less as she held him.

Wyatt knew the feeling. He was cold too.

"I'm tempted to lose my pants. My top half is so much warmer," Imogen mumbled.

No action since yesterday so he had no idea what her panties looked like. They could be the red lace skimpy ones he liked... Bad for tree-sitting.

"The bark is rough. Especially on waterlogged flesh." He wrung out her shirt as best he could, and though it was in no way sterile, it was the only thing he had to apply pressure with. After folding it and placing it over the cut, he held it in place with his knee while he shed his own shirt. Another brief maneuver, and he had her and Michael against his chest, adding to the heat and allowing him to hold pressure to her back with the arm that went around them. "Do you have your waterproof cellphone, by chance?"

Imogen felt around on the thigh pocket of her scrubs, tore the Velcro flap back and handed the phone to him.

A few seconds later, he reached 911 and began barking orders, hurrying the rescue with directions to where they were, the nature of the injuries and Michael's propensity for seizures.

"They'll hurry, right?" she whispered, her teeth chattering less.

The little guy shifted against Wyatt and then scooted to where the adult bodies met and huddled in. He sniffled, still scared, but warmer and obviously feeling safer there with them. "They'll be here soon," Wyatt said, patting Michael's head. "Don't worry, buddy. We'll get you back with your mama soon."

"I'm scared." She must be to admit it. "Tell me about something. Tell me about the cabin."

His arm tightened around her, and she hissed in a breath. Too much pressure on the wound. "Sorry. Cabin. Right." The cabin was about the last thing on his mind right now. He had to search for something to say. "The porch will wrap around." Rubbing Michael's back as he spoke, he tried to warm him more. "Swing. Rocking chairs for warm summer nights, for watching the lightning bugs, listening to the whippoorwills. Crickets. Frogs in the creek."

"No creek talk," Imogen muttered. "What else?"

"Big bedroom. Old clawfoot tub in the bathroom for hot baths."

"Oh, I want a hot bath."

"Loft for other rooms. Windows that open like shutters."

"And a fancy door," Imogen whispered. "Brass fixtures."

"And a fancy door," he agreed, looking at the sky as the sun ducked behind a cloud. Dammit. "Lead crystal too. Maybe stained glass."

"Needs a big mantel for the fireplace."

"Sure does. Where else we going to hang stockings?"

Imogen closed her eyes, rubbing her cheek against the top of Michael's head. She could imagine it all. Nighttime, a roaring fire, stockings hanging above it, and the only other light coming from the twinkle lights on the tree. She whispered, "You like Christmas, Michael?"

He didn't seem inclined to talk. At least when he was crying she knew he was hanging in there. "Do you know Santa, Michael?"

"Ho-ho," he answered, but the weakness in his voice terrified her. She opened her eyes and looked at him. "Wyatt?"

"He's cold," Wyatt said, and maneuvered Imogen

so her back and the shirt compress were against the trunk and he could rouse the little guy. He pulled the boy to his chest and enfolded him completely, both arms wrapped around the tiny body until Michael grew more animated. Large hands rubbed his back and legs briskly where he could reach them.

"Ho-ho. I like that name for him." Imogen cupped her hands, blew in them until they were warmer and placed them in any bare areas. Between the two of them, soon his tiny body had warmed up enough to shake again.

The sound of beating rotors split the air.

"Chopper," Wyatt said. "About time. Michael, you know what we're going to do? We're going to fly in a helicopter. And they will have warm blankets. And they'll take us inside where we can have...cake. And...hot cocoa."

Imogen almost laughed. Cake. Just what every kid wanted when he was terrified and freezing.

Within minutes, the helicopter was hovering above them and a rescuer was descending on a cable to retrieve them.

"Michael first," Imogen insisted. The rescuer explained the harness to Wyatt, but Imogen couldn't focus on it. Her fear had crested when they'd heard the rotors, and with the adrenaline surge now fading she found it harder to keep her eyes open.

"Stay awake, Imogen," Wyatt ordered. Loudly. Once they had Michael strapped to the rescuer's chest, he turned to give her a shake. "Wake up, or I'm going to be angry. Wake up."

Wyatt pulled her against him and the compress from her back and began working the harness on her legs and around her back.

It was okay to sleep now, she thought. Wyatt would take care of everything, even if he was angry.

The last Imogen knew, she was dangling shirtless from a line ascending to a helicopter.

Wyatt squished as he walked, each step announcing he was much soggier than a man wanted to be when surrounded by his peers. Or in October.

The rescuers had given him a shirt and, after stripping Imogen, wrapped warming blankets around the lot of them. He'd shrugged out of his before getting off the chopper, but Michael was still wrapped in his and Imogen in hers on her gurney while they wheeled through the corridors of the emergency department.

Her eyes were open again. She still looked kind of out of it.

"You slipped out there for a little bit," Wyatt said to her, having explained that twice when she'd roused in the helicopter during the flight. She kept forgetting, or she hadn't heard him.

"I remember," she mumbled, lifting one hand touch him. "Michael? You warm now?"

He lay against Wyatt's chest, and looked content to stay there. Wyatt rubbed his back again and answered for him. "He's doing good." He'd given his orders to the flight crew to radio ahead and two curtained bays waited for them. Michael was his patient, Imogen was his nurse. He'd treat them both.

Two beds waited for them, and he stood back as they transferred Imogen to a bed, laying her face-down so he could work on her back. "Warm saline, please. Clean her wound." He set Michael on the bed beside Imogen's and unwrapped him. Looked again for any sign of trauma. Bruises could take a while to form. "Vitals for both."

As soon as Michael realized Wyatt wasn't going to pick him right back up, he started to scream again.

"It's okay, buddy. See, Emma-Jean's here too."

Snagging a stethoscope, he got it in his ears and picked Michael up again so he'd stop crying long enough for him to listen to his lungs without piercing his eardrums. "He sounds good. Get him something to drink. Lukewarm hot chocolate, if you've got it." He handed the little guy to a nurse, "Don't put him down." He thought for a second and added, "Unless he stiffens. Then get him on the floor fast."

The nurse looked surprised but nodded.

Imogen's back and the wound was clean. And they had a line in her. "Did I lose that much blood?"

"Not giving you blood, honey. Just fluids right now." Wyatt patted her head and then stepped to the sink to wash and glove. "Going to piggyback some antibiotics. You're not allergic to anything, right?"

"Sulfa." She mumbled the answer and added, "I want pink sutures."

Wyatt grinned at her. "They're not going to show."

"Pink bandage, then."

He rattled off the antibiotic order to the nurse and got started. "I'll see what I can do."

"Or purple."

"All right, purple." It was good to hear a little of her usual spunkiness return with the fluids.

After numbing the area, he set about stitching it. He'd pulled short stints in Emergency when picking a specialty, but he didn't stitch that much these days. He practiced the motion a couple times before getting started. "Hold real still for me."

"Michael okay?"

Wyatt leaned down and whispered, "I gave him to the bustiest nurse in the area. He's having a snuggle, and drinking hot chocolate from a sippy cup."

"I want to stay until Emily and Nate get here," she said. Already making demands.

"You're spending the night."

"I feel gross. I want a shower." More demands. She liked being in control as much as he did.

"Complain, complain. Haven't you ever been in a flood before?" She shuddered and he grimaced. A step too far. "Let me get this done first." It wouldn't be the way he'd like to shower with her, but they could all use some cleaning up. "And you need to be a little steadier before we brave the shower."

She grumbled something but he missed it, concentrating on the stitching and on Michael.

An hour later, the toddler was asleep, curled up

with a sleeping Imogen. Wyatt really wanted to climb into the bed with them.

Imogen opened her eyes, surprising him. "I felt you looking at me."

"I'm wondering if we can get away with leaving him asleep in a bed and going to the shower."

She stroked Michael's head, which was pillowed on her arm, but he didn't stir. "Where's that nurse who was holding him? I'm not going to go anywhere until someone is holding him. He'll be scared if he wakes up alone."

"I'll see what I can do." Wyatt went in search of the nurse and whatever plastic and tape he could get his hands on to keep Imogen's bandage dry. And to borrow some scrubs. And slippers. Rugged, manly hospital slippers.

CHAPTER ELEVEN

THEY SLEPT IN a pile on the hospital bed—Wyatt on the bottom with Imogen and Michael anchored to him on each side. That soaked clump of people from the top of the tree, transplanted to a dry, safe hospital bed.

That was until Wyatt snuck off to retrieve the bus and the Petersons, leaving Imogen on Michael duty.

The morning after the flood the toddler was remarkably subdued and also quite hungry. They took breakfast together, Michael nestled against Imogen's side with her spooning oatmeal with fruit into him. And when they had finished, he helped her with her scrambled eggs and toast.

A nurse came to give Michael a bath, and that created a bit of drama. Imogen couldn't do everything for him, as she would have liked to. Her back hurt much more today and every little stretch felt like her stitches were popping.

They weren't, of course. A man who dove into flood waters and risked his life to save those who mattered to him wouldn't do a slipshod job of their aftercare. They had to be better than the stitches she'd done for him.

That leap, though. That had bought him something else. Her trust. And her ability to see the possibility of a future together.

Whatever rough areas he had, and no matter how many masks he had yet to produce, she trusted that none of them would hurt her. At least, not on purpose. He might brood like an Olympian, he might keep all kinds of info about his past in a nuclear-blast-survivable vault, but the only skeletons he had were linked to regret. Not putrid, decaying ghosts of relationships past.

She munched some crackers and lay back in the bed, waiting for Michael to return, waiting for Wyatt to return, and had the first urge in weeks to email her parents.

Wyatt had been right about her from their first night together: she didn't have to leave at a predetermined time. She loved him and it was okay to stick around, to improvise. Try to make a life for herself with people who cared about her. Time to take the chance he wanted her to take.

And time to patch up her relationship with her parents. Maybe they'd come and visit for a couple months.

His practice on wheels now also qualified as a flood-defeating super-bus. Wyatt made it through the lower and now mostly still floodwaters around noon, the Petersons with him since no other vehicle could yet make it through the water that topped the only bridge in and out of Bent Reed.

By the time they got to the hospital, Imogen and Michael had drifted into naptime.

Wyatt touched her hand to wake her up and a minute later, with the help of the boy's parents, Emily and Nate replaced Imogen in the bed with their son.

He shook out another gown for her to wear like a robe, and shuffled her off to a nearby empty room for privacy. He needed to check on that wound.

"How you feeling?"

"It hurts like mad today, but I feel pretty good other than that. I think the pain pills are making me fuzzy, though," Imogen murmured, though she didn't slur her words.

Wyatt pulled the curtain shut and gestured for her to turn around. With one hand he moved the gowns out of the way and gently pulled back the bandage to reveal the gash. "No increased redness or drainage. Looks good." He pressed the bandage back in place and resisted the urge to hug her. "The pain isn't due to infection. Just normal healing. But there's good news, I'm going to discharge you and get us home. Sound good?"

Imogen nodded, and took the hugging matter into her own hands, stepping forward to lay her cheek against his shoulder as her arms crept around his middle. Her face burrowed into his shoulder.

Careful of her wound, he held her a little while. "Still okay?"

"Yeah. A little weird, but nothing like a little life-or-death action to put things into perspective."

What did that mean? How in the world could he be so attuned to every little aspect of her demeanor and still have no idea what she was getting at?

"If it doesn't kill you, it makes you stronger?" Guess. Use clichés and platitudes.

"Or something," she said, taking a deep breath and nuzzling closer. She wasn't usually a hugger. So she was definitely still pretty shaken up from the flood. Not that he could blame her. It was probably the scariest thing he'd ever experienced too.

"Want to change out of this gown? I brought your bag in."

"Oh, bless you." She stepped back and sat on the bedside chair while he fetched her clothes and then helped her get changed. Physical needs he could take care of. Jobs that needed doing, he could do.

Discharge papers completed and farewells said, he did what he could: helped her onto the bus and headed for home.

Wyatt got her to Amanda's and settled on the couch with blankets, pillows, the remote, the phone, her laptop, her medicine, something to drink, some munchies and then stood back and gestured to the door. "You should do as little as possible. And I told Aunt Jo that you might ring next door if you need anything."

"You're not staying?" she asked, her brows pinched.

Wow. Invited to stay? The flood must have really shaken her up. "You mean... What do you mean? I can stay a little while if you want."

"No. I mean tonight. I thought maybe you'd stay tonight."

Definitely still shaken up. Wyatt didn't know what to say immediately. This was boyfriend territory, not fling stuff. She wasn't well enough for their usual bedroom activities.

So, she wasn't ready to be alone. Okay. Not a big deal for him. It just seemed out of character for her. "I can stay. I just didn't think you'd want me to."

"Oh." Imogen looked down a moment and then fiddled with the remote she held, television not yet turned on. A fidget. "I have been thinking about that. Me not usually wanting that." The bravery he knew her for faltered and she started smoothing the blanket over her leg repeatedly. "I don't want to not want you to not want to stay." She squinted, replaying the words in her mind, and then tried again. "I want you to want to stay and I want to want to have you stay and want to stay." She sighed, her eyes closing. Frustrated.

And a little stoned besides. It could be the drugs talking.

"Well, I'll stay tonight and tomorrow you'll be feeling more like yourself."

"No." Imogen took another run at the elusive thought. "I want you to stay and I want to want you to stay. Oh. And I want to stay. Here. I want to try and stay here. Like you said. I don't have to decide to go. I can give this a chance and see how we go. How it goes with us."

Us.

"Imm, when I said that you could play it by ear, I was talking about you having a home."

"I know. I want that too. We survived a flood together. Laundry and grocery shopping and Christmases can't be harder."

Hell.

Should he wait until she was better to have this conversation? That would mean playing along and that would probably lead her on if she seriously wanted them to stay together. Move beyond fling. A desire he didn't share.

"I care about you, and I want you to be happy. I think you could be happy living here, staying around Amanda. And we're friends. Friends who are having a fling. Right?" He tap-danced through the words, watching her sober a little from the concentration it took to put together what he was saying. "We'll talk about it tomorrow, okay?"

"You don't want me," she filled in. No talking tomorrow. "I thought…that the you who went into the water was the real you. Don't know why I thought that now."

"It was the real me. I'm always being the real me."

"No. You can't be the you who yelled at Emily

and the you who jumped into the water at the same time. That day with Michael, one second you were this wonderful man who hunted down a little squeaky toy for his patient to use for therapy, and then you were this shouting angry man who made me want to run for cover."

Wyatt scowled. "Those were extenuating circumstances. And it was about the subject, not about me."

"What subject? I know two things: your brother died, and your father blamed you for it. The only inkling I have that you feel wrongly accused by your father is how you snapped at Emily. And those two things I know because someone *other than you* told me."

"And I made up for it."

"I'm so stupid." She shook the remote and then cracked herself lightly on the head with it.

"Stop that." Wyatt stepped forward, taking the device from her.

"I make the same bad decisions over and over and over. Same thing. I was so sure I knew Scott. And then after the flood I thought I finally understood something you'd been telling me. But you didn't mean that."

She stopped looking at him and leaned forward

to grab her purse, from which she fished that stupid little cheese crock and stared at it. If she hit herself on the head with that, he definitely had to stay tonight. He waited, with no idea what to say yet.

"I was supposed to remember that." Imogen rubbed her head with one hand, still examining the crock with a glazed look. "Because I've told you all about my past. You know the things that have hurt me. You know why I keep moving. You know everything about me!"

"Was I asleep when you told me about that stupid little pot you take everywhere?"

Would she even remember this conversation tomorrow?

Imogen stood and wobbled over to him, thrusting the little stoneware container into his hands. "You want this? Here. Take it. And here's the reason I keep it around: it's a reminder. But I will have a fourteen-foot scar on my back to remind me in the future. I can let it go. And I can let you go." Her hands free, she shoved him toward the door. "Get out. Go chainsaw something."

He looked at the ceramic thing in his hand and turned to head out. No goodbyes. Just space and air. And a stop at Jolene's to ask his aunt to check on the raging patient later.

Wyatt climbed into his truck and slammed the door.

Sure. Cheese as a reminder. Of what? To eat plenty of dairy?

He sighed, flipping it around to see if the words printed on the side gave any clue. *Forward.* The only writing on the thing beside the state name and a year printed beneath a coat of arms.

Right.

He flipped the latch and opened the lid. Inside nestled a worn newspaper clipping. He fished it out and began reading. Obituary. Scott Williams.

Scott.

Her ex was dead?

He read on. The phrase "life taken by his own hand" leapt out at him.

What the hell kind of newspaper gave suicide as a cause of death in an obituary?

He flipped it over and looked at a date scrawled on the back, then did the math. About eighteen at the time. God. She must blame herself. The abusive psycho went so far to punish her for leaving him that he'd killed himself?

What had she said? *Guilt can eat you alive. Strip everything from you.*

Damn. And she'd said he knew everything about her. He folded the clipping up and put it back into the little jar.

Part of him wanted to storm back into the house and shake some sense into her, but with the meds she was on that wouldn't do much good. And which face would she credit with that action?

Angry Boyfriend Face. Only he wasn't her boyfriend.

Fling. Angry Fling Man Face. Whatever.

With a deep sigh he dropped the jar into the cup holder and started the truck.

Go chainsaw something.

Gladly.

The gravel drive leading up the mountain had lots of fresh tire tracks when Wyatt pulled in. He was gearing himself up to kick someone's ass when five different vehicles with Harlan County tags came into view. Back on the hill, eleven men worked on his cabin. Three of them he recognized. One approached.

"Nate." Wyatt couldn't think of anything to say but the man's name, and held out one hand.

"Decided to come give you a hand with your cabin. How's Imogen?" Nate shook his hand.

"Recovering." Wyatt didn't want to lie, but he didn't want Nate feeling bad either—his family had been through enough. "How's Michael?"

"He's doin' real good. Hospital's letting him home tomorrow. Left Emily and our moms with him so we could get on up here and give you a hand." He gestured behind him to the cabin. Like Wyatt, Nate didn't so much as glance at the big blue bus. "Got my dad, brothers, Emily's brothers and a few cousins. We wanted to do something nice for you and Imogen."

Wyatt swallowed, more touched by this man's kindness than he knew how to express. Imogen had forced her help on him with the cabin, and after he'd got used to it, it had felt good to not have to tackle the big job on his own. And now he understood how good it felt to have people offer help. Just because he was the last Beauchamp around it didn't mean he had to rebuild alone.

"I appreciate it, Nate. Anyone built a cabin before? If there are better ways, I'm happy to change things, as long as you guys are willing to let me lend a hand."

His home might actually get completed before

winter. Hell, seeing they'd already set half of the logs before he'd got there, his cabin might even have a roof before the day was over.

Two days had passed since the rescue team had pulled them from the tree. One day since she'd basically shoved Wyatt out the door, and it was only now that she felt like her thoughts could be put into some kind of order.

She bent over her case of collectibles and stroked her fingers over the cold surfaces of the largely ceramic mementos. Funny how they all looked so much alike to her now. Probably all came from one company—a knick-knack for every state.

She'd said she could let it go, but it was very weird to have her cheese crock missing from the collection.

And the obituary inside. She winced. Maybe he wouldn't open it. Or maybe he wouldn't notice the cause of death...

Staying away from him for the next three months would be miserable. Impossible if she kept working for him. She should give him a week to find a replacement. And not hang out at night or talk in the bus or...anything else.

Sleeping in the same bed always violated her

rules. But huddling together with him and a scared toddler in a hospital bed had obliterated them. She should've known how it would go if she decided to stay with him. Well, she was going to try and stay anyway. Find a job in Piketon. She could be in the area and never run into him so long as she didn't go near the bus or the mountain.

She was kidding herself if she thought she could work beside him in a closed space for a week without dragging him back to her bed. No matter what he'd once said about building a tolerance for it, it hadn't happened yet. And she'd long ago learned the value of physical closeness to keep emotional needs at bay.

And she would never have believed Wyatt to be impulsive enough to go into the creek after her. Or that he'd risk himself for her.

A knock sounded at the door and she hastily closed the door on her collectibles to head for the front door. A voice outside called her name.

A woman's voice.

Jolene…

Imogen tore the door open. "Amanda?"

"Baby's comin'," Amanda's mother announced, snapping her fingers at Imogen to follow. "How long…?"

"Just a few minutes," Jolene answered before Imogen had gotten the question out.

"So we have time to stop…" This part of Appalachia was peppered with fast talkers. A version of a Southern drawl mingled with the impatience of the North. She needed to talk faster to keep Jolene from repeatedly cutting her off.

"No, I mean the contractions are a few minutes apart. We gotta leave now."

"Why didn't someone come tell me earlier?" A few minutes! Imogen grumbled, cramming her feet into her shoes, which rested by the door with her purse and keys. She locked up and followed.

Amanda was already sitting in the backseat of Jolene's large sedan. Imogen crawled in beside her, taking her hand as Amanda breathed her way through a contraction.

"We wanted you to rest until it was closer to the time."

Imogen nodded. They were trying to respect her space. Even today. Amanda was too good a friend.

"Okay. Back to the hospital! Baby's coming!" Imogen put on her happy face. It was a happy occasion, and she wouldn't let Wyatt mess it up for Amanda. Or for her. "Look at you and your cervix of steel. Keeping that kid in until it was time."

Wyatt would want to know.

Jolene could be the one to call him.

A full clock rotation later, Wyatt made it to the hospital and Amanda's room. Everyone inside was sleeping except for Imogen. Jolene slept on the couch, Amanda in her bed, and Imogen sat beside the bed, rocking the sleeping baby in her arms. She was so engrossed in looking at the little face that she didn't notice him standing in the darkened room.

She loved the little ones.

Was she still mad at him? He'd kind of broken up with her, so probably.

She glanced at him and back to the baby. When she made as if to rise, Wyatt stepped over and put a hand on her shoulder to ease her back.

He knelt beside her chair and looked at the baby swaddled in blue. She smelled good. He'd missed her. A lot.

"You got the message," Imogen whispered, keeping her voice down to keep from waking anyone. She still looked tired.

"I was working. Didn't check messages until this morning." And he'd been glad his cellphone didn't work. It had kept him from calling, texting, or otherwise starting something inadvisable. He gestured around the room with his head. "Everyone all right?"

"This little guy—seven pounds, nine ounces. Picture of health." She gave a report, the details everyone wanted and he hadn't asked for. "Amanda did great. They're all doing just fine."

"And how are you?" He looked at her face, willing her to look him in the eye, even though he knew her opinion of him wasn't the greatest right now. He wanted her to connect with him again. She didn't succumb to his will.

"I'm fine. Been a long few days." Imogen drew a deep breath and then nodded to the baby in her arms. "You can hold him if you like."

"I'll wait. She hasn't named him yet?"

"Not yet. She's struggling with it. Shoots down every suggestion."

They were all struggling with something, except for this little nameless baby cousin. He changed the subject. "I didn't bring the gift. Figured she'd have enough to take home. Left it at Jolene's on the way."

He drew a deep breath and leaned forward to give the baby's head a little kiss. He wanted to kiss the woman holding the baby, or just confirm she was okay. He hadn't expected her to get hurt and he didn't like it one bit. Since she'd failed to succumb to his will, he touched her leg to make her look at him. "Will you come by the mountain when everyone's settled?"

Imogen had been bolder when she hadn't known him, charging his mountain and making demands. And now she held his gaze, but there was wariness in those beautiful blue eyes. "I don't think I'm up to building or hauling logs right now."

"No, I wanted to show you something. No heavy lifting required."

"I guess so." She looked back at the baby, who was stirring and scowling.

Wyatt stood, looking at Amanda and Jolene. "Don't want to wake them. I should get back to the mountain."

"I'll tell them you came by and left a gift at Jolene's," Imogen said, looking up at him.

Wyatt reached down, stroked her hair back from her face and kissed her forehead, much as he had the baby's. "Get some rest when Jolene wakes up. You're still injured."

Get in. Get out. Go home.

But he was all out of things to chainsaw.

* * *

The hospital was about forty minutes' drive from the mountain. Forty minutes of thinking time. Forty minutes to make some decisions. Or to realize he had to make some decisions.

He pulled up the gravel incline to the mountain and past his dad's bus to park. The cabin greeted him. And now that it was a reality, another notion became abundantly clear: he didn't want to live in the cabin alone. Nate's family might not have much money, but they all pulled together to help one another out, and they genuinely liked doing it.

It was nice seeing a family—any family—on the mountain again.

He could see why his father had never rebuilt the cabin once Mom and Josh were gone. The bus looked almost homey by comparison.

That thing had to be gone before he turned into his father.

With a deep breath he climbed out of the truck and headed for the old rust heap.

Just go inside. Get it over with. Quick, like ripping off a bandage.

Unlike the last time she'd dreaded going to the mountain, Imogen dressed easily and arrived on time. No food to make. No trying to figure out what to wear. Just herself, and the nagging suspicion that today would be her last visit to the mountain.

The rain moved past the day of the flood, and since then, everything had dried up enough to make the drive up the mountain possible.

No spinning tires.

No slinging mud.

No blue bus.

Imogen blinked as she pulled past the big rectangle of dead grass where the bus had sat.

Her second shock of the day came a few seconds later when she noticed that the cabin was more or less finished. The walls were all up. There was even some kind of wooden roof in place, covered over with a blue tarp. And a beautiful door covered with ornate carving, lead glass and brass fixtures. Better than any she'd pictured.

Wyatt sat on a cast-off log that had failed to become part of the cabin.

She rolled the car to a stop at the foot of the rise on which the cabin sat, and parked beside his truck. Wyatt stood and tucked his hands in his pockets.

He looked good. Clean. Freshly groomed. Flannel had never looked so good on anyone.

She climbed the short distance and gestured to the cabin. "That's a mighty fancy door you've got there."

"Thought you might like to see it," Wyatt said, watching her approach. She was still pale. "How's your back?"

"It's okay," she said, not looking at him. "Where are the windows that open like shutters?" Apparently, it was easier to talk about the cabin.

"Ordered," Wyatt said, reaching up to wipe sweat from his brow. It was October, not August, and he was sweating.

"There's no holes for them."

"You build the box and then cut out places for the windows and door."

"I see." She really wasn't going to make this easy on him. "How did—?"

"Nate." He liked it better when she wouldn't shut up. This quiet version of Imogen drew attention to the tension between them. "When I got here on Thursday, they were already working."

"They? Who came?"

"He dragged every able-bodied man in his family up here. There were a dozen of us. And it turns out we were doing it wrong. They had to take everything apart and fix it." He offered his elbow. "Want to see inside?"

"I do." Did she really? So sedate, and she looked him in the eye so little...he couldn't really be sure what she was thinking. Still mad at him? Probably.

"Plumbing and power will have to come after the roof is done, then the porch." He stepped up into the cabin and reached for her other hand, much as he had the first day on the last step up the mountain. She was slower to take his hand now. "Watch your step, the cinder blocks are wobbly."

She released her hold as soon as she was inside and surveyed the unfinished plywood floor and the rough walls, but once her gaze found the fireplace, it stayed.

"It's better than I pictured. You should sleep in here now, even unfinished. Warmer than the tent."

"I have." Wyatt gestured to his sleeping bag in the corner on the old steamer trunk he'd brought from the bus.

"Good. Good. Have you had a fire?"

"Not yet. Have to make sure the chimney is fire-ready." And he'd been very busy. Working himself into a lather so he wouldn't think about her and the sadness in her unfocused eyes when she'd said those four words. *You don't want me.*

"Thank you for showing it to me. I'm sure it will be beautiful when it's all done. It already looks great." She turned away from him abruptly and headed for the door. Wyatt caught up with her with a couple of big steps, long enough to get hold of her hand as she went back down the wobbly steps.

"There's one more thing, if you can stay a little longer."

She looked at him and then shrugged. "Okay." He saw her look at where the bus had been, and then discard the idea of asking about it.

"Let's take the four-wheeler."

"Where?"

"Up the mountain." Wyatt led her over to the vehicle and climbed on, then gestured in front of him. "You're still wounded. Rather you sat in front of me so I know I won't topple you off."

She frowned and looked up the mountain. "Why are we going up the mountain?"

"There's something you want to see."

"The foliage?"

He didn't want to lie, but that was part of it. Her reticence didn't give him much confidence for how his plan might turn out though. "The leaves are at peak color..."

A moment later she straddled the four-wheeler with Wyatt behind her, locked in the cage of his arms and the handlebars.

"Lean back." He slid her against his frame, then started the engine and began a weaving path up the mountainside, eventually reaching a low-gradient trail that wound across the steep incline to the ridge at the very top.

Once they topped the ridge, he angled the machine toward the graveyard.

The vehicle rolled to a stop. He climbed off and offered her a hand.

Imogen wiggled her hand free, intent on hiding it in her pocket, but he caught her fleeing hand, guided it to his elbow and kept the other hand wrapped over it. His touch was going to do her in. Any second now tears would escape, regardless of her wishes. The worst kind of emotional blackmail. "Wyatt..."

"Wait. I need to say some things." He didn't release her hand, but drew her toward the blocks.

The graves inside the wall had never been tended. Massive trees grew from the centers of graves. Big, well-fed trees. Somehow that didn't weird her out. It seemed right, like it kept these people alive. Like they were part of the mountain they'd all lived on. The headstones—some of which were so covered with moss the names couldn't be made out—sat more or less where they'd been placed however many centuries past, now many at the feet of these tall, thick trees.

Except for three new graves outside the wall with modern headstones. They looked out of place and yet right at the same time. She read the names: Anson, Elizabeth and Joshua Beauchamp. The years etched into the latter sucked the air right out of her. "He was only seven."

"Diagnosed at five. Leukemia," Wyatt said, still holding her hand to his elbow. His fingers tightened a touch, in concert with the tension in his voice. It was still hard to talk about.

"How old were you?"

"Eleven when he was diagnosed. Thirteen when he passed."

Imogen felt tears on her cheeks and the warmth of his touch spreading up her arm. She was afraid to hope, but he was sharing his secrets. "And you were his carer?"

"Mom died when he was about Michael's age,

and Dad was always working. I knew something was wrong, but it took me a few months to realize how sick he was. I was in full-blown denial."

It was no stretch to understand he'd have blamed himself for not spotting that. But what Mr. Shoemaker had said to her came back to her and she turned a little to look at him. "Your father blamed you for it."

"He did. I did too. I tried to make up for it somehow, but you can't really make that kind of thing up. All that is a long story, but the short version is that when I graduated I realized there could never be peace between us. So when I got a chance to go to college out of state, I went. Never came back until his funeral. Then I couldn't bring myself to leave."

"Because you love the mountain," Imogen said softly, understanding. She loved the mountain too. This serene spot. The view. She couldn't think of a better spot to spend eternity.

"It's my home. No matter where I went, I never felt part of anything until I came home again."

"Are you still mad at him?" Imogen felt like she belonged too. The patients who had seemed so foreign to her had only taken a little while to understand, and as soon as she'd made the effort, they'd welcomed her. Amanda had welcomed her. Jolene. Wyatt.

"After I left the hospital the other day, I realized I needed to deal with the bus. It was like every instinct told me it was time to go inside. And it was enlightening."

"Enlightening?" she prompted, stepping a little closer, so their arms didn't make a wide V between them.

"I dug into the steamer trunk and went through some boxes with pictures, and a photo album from when Josh was a baby. The pictures of my dad..." He shook his head, and it clearly took an effort for him to wrestle these words out, but he had to figure out what to tell her without her prompting him.

"He was smiling. Happy. Sober. It felt like I was looking at photos of someone I didn't remember. The man I remember had been eaten alive by grief and guilt. He was a man who wasn't able to protect his family or the woman he loved." He cleared his throat and carried on louder than he had been speaking up to that point. "I remembered what that felt like. That feeling made me jump into the water."

He loved her. He *loved* her. He'd said it. Indirectly, but the volume and the glancing blow at the confession had to count for something.

"We didn't speak for nearly twenty years, but that wasn't all his fault. Part of it was mine. I grew up. I could have made a different decision, but we were both too stubborn and too hurt to think of anyone else." He stepped closer, and brushed her hair behind her ear. "I'm not making that same mistake with you. I read the obituary."

She nodded, her heart in her throat, scrambling for something to say.

"It said suicide," Wyatt prompted.

"It's not true," Imogen babbled, and then realized she needed to come clean with him too. "I only kept one of the obituaries. The first one. It said suicide. It hit me hardest. Everything got more confusing after that."

"What do you mean?"

"He didn't kill himself. He told me he was going to when I left, and I was mad at him and so hurt by everything. I used the weapon I knew how to use. I told him to use pills because it would leave the least mess for his mother to clean up."

Wyatt winced.

If anything should make him have second thoughts about her... A chill danced over her body.

Imogen swallowed and looked down. "After we moved and I got settled, I still worried about him. I thought he loved me in his own twisted way, so I wrote to see how he was. The only response I got was that obituary in an envelope."

Just keep going. Get it out. She drew a deep breath and talked as fast as she could. One breath. Say it, say all of it. "And then a week later I got another one. Different. And then another. And another. He was having a friend at the paper print them. So they all looked legit. But after the first month we figured out it was him and I called."

Two breaths, and more rapid-fire words. "My mouth. My mouth made things worse. We tried to get the police involved. It didn't work. Not until he started sending packages with bloody razor blades. That made the police take it seriously. He had some kind of psychotic breakdown and has been in and out of institutions since then."

Wyatt tilted her chin up, his own expression incredulous. "Imm...that's not love. That's mental illness."

"It could be both," Imogen said, then sucked in another couple of breaths, trying to slow down her racing pulse.

"Guilt will eat you alive if you let it." Wyatt's

murmured words echoed snippets of conversations they'd had. He released her chin and slid his arms around her. She leaned against him, but fear kept her from holding him. Her fingers curled uselessly in the sides of his shirt. "What does the jar remind you of?"

"I should've left sooner, even if I loved him. The longer I stayed, the worse it got. I prolonged it when it would have been more humane to end it. My pride kept me from telling my parents that settling down was going so badly. I'd whined for years, every time we'd moved somewhere new. But if I'd left earlier…" Imogen didn't know how to make him understand better than that. "Sometimes I feel like I barely survived him."

"That's because you didn't, sweetheart." He rubbed her back, above the wound, to the other side of the wound, ever conscious of her injury.

Of course she'd survived. She was alive. Even after the flood water had nearly done her in.

"The girl who wanted a home and family enough to let her parents leave her behind?" Wyatt stepped back and handed the crock to her, but left his long square fingers wrapped over hers. "Are you sure she survived? It looks to me you're carrying around her urn."

Her hands tingled beneath his. Her throat burned. And for all the speed and force with which she breathed, it didn't feel like her lungs were doing their job.

"Imogen." When he said her name, she looked up, away from the joined hands holding the ridiculous crock. "Let it go. Today is a good day to lay her to rest. Here. And you stay with me."

Tears spilled over.

Wyatt released her hand long enough to retrieve a hand spade from the four-wheeler and held it out to her.

Could it be that simple?

"No more scary masks. I think the only time my reactions bother you is when I'm angry. Or distant."

She nodded after a moment. "I… Yes."

"I don't think that guy is going to be around much anymore. He was lonely and too proud to ask for help." He rubbed his hands on his pants. Sweaty palms? And he looked so certain. "I saw you holding the baby, and I wanted it to be ours. The cabin is almost finished, but I don't want to live there if you're not with me."

She wanted to live in the cabin too.

"Just lay our old hurts in the dirt and let them go?" Imogen tried the words out.

"Then we don't have to worry about them anymore," Wyatt answered.

Imogen hefted the spade in one hand and looked at the crock in the other. So small a thing compared to the load he'd carried. She knelt beside Josh's tombstone and stabbed the ground. Over and over, she chipped at the rocky soil, loosening it little by little. When she got tired, Wyatt knelt opposite her and took over.

They didn't have to dig a big hole, the little ceramic crock nestled neatly into a fist-size space. With shaking hands, Imogen raked the dirt back in to cover it, tears now rolling down her cheeks. "I feel like I should say something." Her hands still cupped the mounded earth.

Wyatt placed his hands over hers and tilted his head to catch her eye. "Rest in peace, Imogen Donally." And then he smiled, a flirting light in those coal-black eyes. Hope. Love. He had the best smile. "Here with the family of Emma-Jean Beechum."

He made her smile. And then he made her laugh. "Was that a proposal?"

"I thought it was a pretty good one." He leaned

forward and pressed a warm kiss to her lips then nudged a tear off her cheek with his nose.

"It was pretty sneaky," she murmured against his lips. And pretty cute. And made her want to give him a hard time. "You don't even have a ring."

Wyatt leaned back and crammed one hand into a pocket. With whatever he'd extracted hidden in his grip, he reached for her left hand and slid a ring onto her finger. Something dangled from it.

Imogen turned her hand and looked at the key. On the key ring on her ring finger.

"It's for the fancy door," Wyatt whispered.

He had given her a home.

Her eyes welled again. She opened her mouth to say something but her voice went all squeaky and unintelligible. But it didn't seem to matter. He understood.

He drew her into his arms and kissed her cheeks. Then he shifted to the side and produced a diamond ring from his other pocket and swapped it with the key ring.

"What I actually planned on saying was how do you feel about having another name no one ever says right? Emma-Jean Beechum, Imogen Beauchamp...I love them both."

"That one's good." She grinned, swiping the

back of her dirty hand over her tear-slickened cheeks, probably leaving a streak of mud behind. "Should've stuck with the plan."

"Someone told me I should be more relaxed and impulsive."

"What fool told you that?"

"Some woman I used to date, before I got engaged."

"I didn't say yes yet."

"But you will." He rose and pulled her up from the ground with him and into his arms. She wound her arms about his waist under his jacket so she could feel the heat from his skin. He whispered into her hair, "Because we love each other. You love me and I love you. You want to bring a family to this mountain again. With me."

They may have been standing on top of a mountain, with autumn blanketing the rolling hills around them in gold, rust and red, but the best view was hers—right there beneath his chin, tucked inside his oversize jacket. Imogen buried her nose in his collar and breathed him in. Moss, black earth and the sweetness of the forest. He smelled like heaven. "Take me back to our cabin. I have a powerful need to get naked and roll around in your sleeping bag."

Wyatt grinned. "Yes, ma'am." He swept her to the four-wheeler and got her seated, then took the winding path down the mountain.

Imogen announced, "I get to be on top!"

"You can't call dibs on position," he said at her ear.

"Yes, I can."

Hadn't he figured out yet that everyone was happier when they did what she wanted?

She'd just have to spend the next fifty years reminding him.

* * * * *

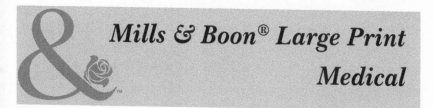

May

GOLD COAST ANGELS: BUNDLE OF TROUBLE	Fiona Lowe
GOLD COAST ANGELS: HOW TO RESIST TEMPTATION	Amy Andrews
HER FIREFIGHTER UNDER THE MISTLETOE	Scarlet Wilson
SNOWBOUND WITH DR DELECTABLE	Susan Carlisle
HER REAL FAMILY CHRISTMAS	Kate Hardy
CHRISTMAS EVE DELIVERY	Connie Cox

June

FROM VENICE WITH LOVE	Alison Roberts
CHRISTMAS WITH HER EX	Fiona McArthur
AFTER THE CHRISTMAS PARTY...	Janice Lynn
HER MISTLETOE WISH	Lucy Clark
DATE WITH A SURGEON PRINCE	Meredith Webber
ONCE UPON A CHRISTMAS NIGHT...	Annie Claydon

July

HER HARD TO RESIST HUSBAND	Tina Beckett
THE REBEL DOC WHO STOLE HER HEART	Susan Carlisle
FROM DUTY TO DADDY	Sue MacKay
CHANGED BY HIS SON'S SMILE	Robin Gianna
MR RIGHT ALL ALONG	Jennifer Taylor
HER MIRACLE TWINS	Margaret Barker

Mills & Boon® Large Print

Medical

August

TEMPTED BY DR MORALES	Carol Marinelli
THE ACCIDENTAL ROMEO	Carol Marinelli
THE HONOURABLE ARMY DOC	Emily Forbes
A DOCTOR TO REMEMBER	Joanna Neil
MELTING THE ICE QUEEN'S HEART	Amy Ruttan
RESISTING HER EX'S TOUCH	Amber McKenzie

September

WAVES OF TEMPTATION	Marion Lennox
RISK OF A LIFETIME	Caroline Anderson
TO PLAY WITH FIRE	Tina Beckett
THE DANGERS OF DATING DR CARVALHO	Tina Beckett
UNCOVERING HER SECRETS	Amalie Berlin
UNLOCKING THE DOCTOR'S HEART	Susanne Hampton

October

200 HARLEY STREET: SURGEON IN A TUX	Carol Marinelli
200 HARLEY STREET: GIRL FROM THE RED CARPET	Scarlet Wilson
FLIRTING WITH THE SOCIALITE DOC	Melanie Milburne
HIS DIAMOND LIKE NO OTHER	Lucy Clark
THE LAST TEMPTATION OF DR DALTON	Robin Gianna
RESISTING HER REBEL HERO	Lucy Ryder

Discover more romance at

www.millsandboon.co.uk

- ❤ WIN great prizes in our exclusive competitions
- ❤ BUY new titles before they hit the shops
- ❤ BROWSE new books and REVIEW your favourites
- ❤ SAVE on new books with the Mills & Boon® Bookclub™
- ❤ DISCOVER new authors

PLUS, to chat about your favourite reads, get the latest news and find special offers:

- 🔲 Find us on facebook.com/millsandboon
- 🐦 Follow us on twitter.com/millsandboonuk
- ❤ Sign up to our newsletter at millsandboon.co.uk